ROBERT TRIES TO HELP

MIKE PEARSON

To Frances

ONE
ROBERT TRIES TO HELP

WOODVILLE MULTI-DISCIPLINARY
COMMUNITY MENTAL HEALTH TEAM.
08/04/2017 3:30 PM.

An urgent message for he who dares
Our worthy champion of communal cares
Robert and Rosy will fly to the rescue
But best laid plans can flounder, I'll bet you.

'SOD IT,' said Robert. 'Why's he waited till last thing Friday? I bet he's been sitting on it all week.'

'What a life,' scoffed Rosealea. 'Where's your commitment to the recovery ethos all of a sudden?'

'Yeah, but, give us a fighting chance, eh?' He poked at his papers and produced a yellow message, which had been there since Wednesday. 'Ah, right yes. Dr. Pong-Ping reckons the Old Professor's taken a left turn - can we expedite a Mental Health Act assessment and commission a comprehensive risk-profile-schedule type thing while we're at it?'

Rosealea snorted. 'The Old Prof.? He wouldn't hurt a fly. I'd be more concerned about that weirdo assistant he lives with - wears a tassel and carries a girly bag, but maybe I've been a social porker for too long.'

'I'm fond of the old Fess, as well. He fixed my airplane last year when I had a prang in the forest,' said Robert.

His colleague had another snort. 'Are you still getting about in that old thing?'

'Yeah - built to last "Fireflies" are and the Prof did a few special adjustments for me.'

Rosealea gave him a look but held her tongue.

Robert felt on the back foot; he secretly envied Rosealea, her 'Red Balloon', leased from the council at a very attractive rate. It had a tame bird of paradise, trained to detect stress and sing softly to the driver. Fully air-conditioned as standard. He knew she was a lovely Pig, she was a lucky one too.

'What you gonna do then, Robby?'

He stood up and crumbs from a vegetable pasty fell to the floor, some lodged themselves in the turn-ups of his favourite yellow corduroy trousers. 'Right, I'm off to collate perceptions with Willie Mouse. When in doubt, consult your line manager.'

She sniffed as he left the room and began to poke clumsily at a phone.

> Says Willie Mouse this won't lie down
> You'd best get off to Woodville town
> Proactive work will save the day
> So smarten up and on your way.

'I know,' said Robert's boss. 'But we need to be safe rather than sorry; it's been hard for him. Didn't you hear about what happened over there last week?'

'Er, yes - wasn't there some bother, or something? At his castle wasn't it?'

Willie gave him a look and explained the bother to his colleague. 'There was a break-in, aggravated by all accounts, but we know all about them. Right pair of chancers, on ASBOS already - Algy Pig and Bill Badger. Not a brain between them, but they roughed up the old boy, then took off with a secret potion in a bottle with "Secret Potion" stamped on it. It might have been worse, but the Prof.'s companion loosed the little dragon and they legged it. That Algy Pig's a bad bit of goods - I was out for a pint with Joey Parrot from court liaison last week and he reckons this lad accounts for a third of all juvenile crime on his own. Anyway, I think you should go and see how the Professor is - probably got a touch of that post-trauma collywobbles by the sound of it.'

'Yes, I think he will have. Who's the other one ... and you said they'd got their paws on something dodgy?'

'Bill Badger, comes from a rough family, easily led. Like a lot of the stuff the Prof has a hand in, there were unforeseen effects. It had been formulated as a cure for erectile dysfunction in squirrels - all it did was take our two off their feet for seventy-two hours. As a result, Policeman Pelican found them easy to lift.'

After a brief recap of some of the dafter schemes to have come from the Professor's castle over the years - coal you could grow in a garden, magic trousers, etc. - Willie advised Robert to take Rosealea with him on account of her empathy with people like the Professor; Robert was unsure, and asked if she might not be related to 'this Algy'.

'Probably,' said Willie. 'There's a lot of them about.'

'Well, what if I say no?'

'Is that what you're saying?'

'No.'

'Well, that's as good as a yes then.'

Rosealea sighed. 'God, you Bears are all the same; why can't you be more like Pigs? Listen, watch my snout.'

He grabbed his satchel but held his tongue. In his experience of empathy, Rose listening and watching were the least reliable paths to understanding. She pulled on her shawl and fastened a bonnet before boarding his 'rust bucket'.

From a high municipal window, Willie watched his two most experienced workers hunker in Robert's flimsy plane. He knew they'd get there and back in one piece and that the barmy scientist would benefit from their intervention, but what concerned him more were the green shoots he'd spotted of love's uncertain harvest. The last office bunk-up had led to fisticuffs on the steps of County Hall, prurient press interest, and extended sick leave for two. Then again, it had been the married council leader, Glynis Whippet, and 'Pat' Patterdale, a gifted but wayward CPN, who'd ended up doing penance on the wards. He had to concede that Robert's romance had more going for it, though he'd have to step up to the plate with Porky Pig. She was a feisty lass and he was a bit wet when all was said and done. He could imagine her shouting at Robert.

'They were alright when I checked them last week.'

'It's not the planes plugs want looking at, it's yours Herbert.'

He got the engine going and drowned out his passenger as they accelerated down the runway and up into the air. As they circled County Hall, he could see the town, bordered by green hills and dense woodland. Robert felt his mood begin to lift and Rosealea rested a trustful trotter on his commanding arm. Then, a cloud came close.

'Naff off yeller kecks,' cried a hostile voice. It was one of the bad Monkeys from the high-rise hills on the Scrubby Estate.

Robert looked to see a wizened head peering over the edge of the cloud to give more cheek as they passed. 'Don't fancy yours, mate.'

'Little twat,' shouted Rosealea.

'Chubby chaser,' called the Chimp.

'We should find something for these poor youths to do. It's no wonder they end up hoeing a bad row,' observed Robert.

Rosealea didn't hear him but seemed to be thinking along similar lines when she bawled, 'I eat scabby Monkeys to get this size, you little scroat.'

A westerly current carried the cheeky Monkey away from them and Robert rode the winds of fortune towards the Nutbush City limits.

The Old Professor's castle was located beyond the town, just before the terrain that opened out into the Nutbush Valley and then the urban sprawl of new development. The old castle also served as a rest home for clapped-out dogs of the Parish and, as Robert brought them down in the courtyard, he could see a rheumy-eyed Labrador lifting its leg hesitantly against the stone wall.

'You better lead on this,' advised Rosealea. 'He won't be best pleased to see me.'

Robert nodded and looked at one of the barred windows. He thought he saw a furtive shape disappear behind it as they landed.

> *A challenging task for Robert and friend*
> *The Old Professor's gone round the bend*
> *The limits of their social caring*
> *Are stretched by sights a little scaring.*

An arthritic Airedale tottered over to waive a mucky paw at the turret of a dark tower. 'He's up there,' wheezed the Dog.

Robert looked but saw nothing.

The Dog looked to Rosealea but she had taken a sudden interest in the castle walls and had her back to him.

'What's your name?' asked Robert. 'Your face seems familiar to me.'

'I am Tony of Plymouth. You were kind to me when I was re-housed and needed help with my benefit forms.'

Robert remembered and chatted kindly as Tony led them slowly to a concealed door, which opened onto a mechanical carpet set on steam-powered casters.

The Dog bid them good luck and worked a lever that sent them clattering along a dingy passage.

Rosealea had got one on her. 'Your face seems familiar to me,' she sneered. 'You'd do well to tell one of his lot from another, great matted beasts of the bog.'

'Just think eh - diversity training. We embrace difference and value individual strengths.'

'You're having a laugh, you are. You stopped short of embracing Tony of Plymouth and, as for individual strengths, they're ones ready for the knacker's yard. He nearly keeled over as he pointed the way.'

He peered at the carpet as they began to slow down. Sometimes, Rosy seemed to go out her way to undermine his efforts. There were times when he wondered if she was right. They came to a halt then a little man in a blue uniform beckoned them forward and spoke to Rosealea.

'What did he say?'

'Not telling you - not enough diversity.'

Sweet Jesus, thought Robert. If only she knew how hard he'd tried to understand women. The serious talks with Ted Sloth ... he'd even bought a book by Suzie Aardvark, which had delved deep into the pit of despair that was, as Sandmartin Amis had dubbed it, 'the man woman stuff'.

After struggling gamely with Suzie every night for a month,

he came to believe that if you knew the answers you wouldn't have to ask the questions, and, it would be a boring old world if we were all the same.

Rosealea gave him one of her kinder smiles. 'He told me the boss has been off it for weeks but, last week, doings sent him over the edge. He's caught strange sounds and bad smells from the lab. And, last week, the trusted assistant with the tassel nipped out and told him to phone Funny Pong. When the Prof found out, he went ballistic and beat the little bloke with gusto. All very uncharacteristic apparently.'

'With *gusto*?'

'So he says. Anyway, I feel a risk assessment coming on. Do you think we should give Policeman Pelican a heads up ... old Sticky Beak's done a few of these in his time?'

'What about your little friend? Do you think he might help - you know act as an advocate and help us be less restrictive?'

'You mean, get us in to see how bonkers he is?'

'Yes, but let's not bother Policeman Pelican just yet.'

Rosealea turned to the little fellow - Trevor - who had been standing at a distance, patiently smoking an enormous joint. He appeared reluctant, until she whispered something in his ear; then he became keen to help in any way he could.

Robert marveled at how persuasive she could be. Boss Grogan, the salty old day centre manager, had been shouting in Reception the other week over rumoured cuts to services. By the time Rosy had made him tea and sat with him, he'd forgotten what all the fuss was about. Sometimes, you didn't need to understand them, just be glad they were there.

> *A surprise for Robert and Rosealea*
> *When Beppo the monkey makes the tea*
> *The Prof's place smells of furtive brewing*
> *With many a sign of unwise doing.*

Trevor disappeared through a concealed door and the visitors moved over to hear what was going on behind a larger one, beneath a green light. They picked up sounds of conflict and passion; furniture moved across the floor and high expressed emotion heated the air. The green light sparkled, and Trevor peered uncertainly from behind the door.

'He'll see you now,' said the shaken dogs-body and limped back in.

The laboratory was dark and macabre. They glimpsed a small shape scuttle about, then a tired and reedy voice welcomed them. 'It's only Beppo. I'll get him to fix us a drink - would you like tea or coffee, or perhaps some of my new tonic wine?'

'Tea,' they responded without hesitation.

'Very good,' sighed the Prof and nodded to the watchful chimp.

Robert felt sorry for the old boy, hiding away in his gaseous domain with only the monkey for company. He could cheerfully shoot Algy Pig and salt him for bacon. No more soft options for that one if he had anything to do with it.

Rosealea showed her best form by talking nicely to the Professor, seeming to win a frail confidence from him and, gradually, the sorry tale was told.

The two intruders had raised a terrible fright by giving Beppo super strength lager, then tying up his owner with hardy twine, which had been lifted from Robert's father's shed and making him watch the cruel prank. It was only when the plucky dragon had seen them off, and Beppo had sobered up, that he'd been freed, scared out of his wits. He'd refused to leave his lab. And had become increasingly detached from what passed for normality. It finally occurred to his companions that he was more than ordinarily barmy when he'd proposed a live-in arrangement where he could distil brew, or otherwise meet his requirements of daily living without setting foot outside the laboratory.

Treatment and, hopefully, cure were to be provided by Beppo and Trevor, who would learn the entire canon of English literature so they could perform selected classics each evening to comfort their troubled employer. When they'd kicked up over 'The Dream of the Rood', he lost his temper and went after them with a rolled-up copy of his formula for instant toast and marmalade.

It was all very sad and Rosealea produced a clean hanky from her bonnet as Beppo came in with the tea, taking care to stay beyond his master's reach.

The old man noticed. 'See him cower and flinch from me. What have I done? My wits are addled, and the Devil rides out to trick me; oh woe on this house of misrule.'

'Just listen to him,' muttered the monkey as he climbed onto Robert's shoulder.

They moved to a distant part of the room as Rosealea counseled the old Professor. She told him that it was good to talk.

> *A wondrous elixir to cure every need*
> *But the Old Professor hooked on speed?*
> *A sorry outcome as Beppo tells it*
> *Robert must act to calm things down a bit.*

Guided by Beppo, Robert found a fine mess of test tubes, powders, and a wide-ranging stock of herbal material. Beppo switched on his little torch so that Robert could make out a large steel shed sprouting funnels, levers, and other appendages. He wondered what alchemy the Professor had been messing with.

Beppo told him of a recipe read in haste and the chance

production of an amphetamine-based jam when a calmative elixir had been expected. He'd eaten it anyway, but it had turned out to be very moreish and the boss had been hooked after just one round of sandwiches. The resourceful monkey had hidden the rest of the stock and tampered with the masher, so the supply had been blocked.

But the damage had been done to the Prof's equilibrium and there had been no living with him as harsh words and violence came and went, to be replaced by lassitude and the waterworks. He had to be taken away.

Robert was moved by the story but wanted to know where the rest of the Class A preserve was hidden. Beppo smiled for the first time that day and set him a riddle: where would the last place be that he'd expect to find it?

Robert couldn't be bothered and, after a halfhearted stab at Granny Guinea Pig's goody barrel, asked to be told. He was horrified to hear that it had been stashed in his father's allotment shed. This was another bad monkey but they needed his help.

'I think he'll be alright, but we do need to get him off to a safe place. What do you say? You're practically his nearest relative.'

Beppo put him right on that one but had a good idea. Hadn't the Sage of Um just opened a special facility for meditation and such like? Robert should have known about that but was pleased by Beppo's sharpness.

The place has been built with matching lottery funding and had a top-of-the-range unit for challenging cases, where the furniture was bolted down. Robert agreed to commission a cherub who could get a message to the Sage told Beppo to get back in with his boss and prepare to help shift him over there.

The sharp Monkey was having none of it and told Robert he was going to live with the Chinese Emperor as soon as the Prof. was taken away - he had a bigger castle, and Tiger Lily in residence. It was a no-brainer. Robert wondered what might happen to Beausephalus, the little Dragon, and the rest of them.

Beppo reckoned they had already jumped ship or taken refuge in the older, seldom visited parts of the building. While he was about it, he anticipated Robert's next question by telling him where he could submit his carer's assessment. Fair enough thought the social worker, he knew they were pants too.

Rosealea got the nod from Beppo and managed to help the Professor pack a few things for 'his rest' and write up some instructions for Trevor, or whoever else might come out of the woodwork in his absence. It was mostly daft research business, which Rosealea skipped in favour of the practical stuff; she was confident they'd know what was what on the lab side.

The Professor then lapsed into a mode of shuffling cooperation, and it was plain sailing. The three chums were soon standing by 'Firefly', ready for the off. The patient was to travel in a large basket strapped to Robert's fuselage, with Rosealea for company. The ever-efficient Trevor had come up with the arrangement in double-quick time. The take-off was a bit bumpy, but Robert got them up.

Trevor waved them off with a wan grin and as he climbed up and away from the castle, Robert glimpsed a number of wary faces peering back. Awestruck and frayed, they projected an immense collective gratitude. He also noticed how low he was on fuel but decided not to bother anyone with it. There was no helping about that; it was all he could do to remember the way to The Sage's place.

. . .

Fortunately, the gilded Cherub, who'd taken the message appeared by the plane to guide Robert, tooting on his pocket trumpet the while. The pilot felt that he was no Miles Dormouse and was keen to keep him from spotting Rosealea. These common Woodville folks could be a mixed blessing, but since the County Council had required them to get a licence before they could offer services, he'd noticed a change for the better. There had been a time when Cherub shooting had been a popular sport in rougher parts of Nutbush City. Talk in the pubs held that Rosealea's delinquent uncle had a hand in organising 'Pixie Shoots', but nothing was ever proved.

The engine stalled and Robert looked at the fuel gauge, but it was just more turbulence from the basket. He spotted Rosey's shawl flapping behind them and was glad when the Cherub indicated the spot ahead with his compact and shiny horn before he climbed up and away from them.

The Old Professor's safe at last
But Rosealea cries damn and blast
Robert's let her down again
And she's about to cause him pain.

He pulled out all the stops to get them down gently, using all his flying skills and a pair of trusty garden shears he kept handy in the cockpit. He dropped them in the Sage's garden and circled for a safe place to land properly. He had half a mind to open the throttle and head for the clouds, but he was nearly on empty by this time. He came down in a field across the road where a friendly cow offered to keep an eye on 'Fire-fly'. He wanted to talk to linger because he'd seen Rosealea by the front door of the Sage's place but the cow turned away from him as Rosealea called, 'Get 'ere now, you're heading for a slap.'

She looked a right sight in her borrowed gear: scarlet frou-frou, jumble-sale cardie, and purple leg warmers. 'I'm sorry babe. Did he play up then?'

'Did he ever ... still he's not in his right mind, is he. I told The Sage you'd call round on your day off.'

'Fair enough. Fancy a cup of tea? My mum bakes on a Friday.'

'Oh, Robert, you know how to talk to a lady; there'll be a cake in it then?'

Robert was forgiven. He wondered if she'd be up for a pint later at the Todgers Inn. They walked off happily to Robert's parents' house, avoiding the green where Gaffer Jarge hung about frightening children and abusing cherubs. He was just a smelly old man in tights, but he had his rights.

They looked back at him, leering by a tree. 'When I was a kid,' said Rose. 'Our Percy threatened to sell me to old cock-face, said Gaffer were saving up and nearly had the right money, but Percy kept raising the price as I grew.'

'That's emotional abuse. Where is your caring cousin now?'

'In prison for nicking; he'll be getting all kinds of abuse now, the old git.'

Robert began to rehearse a peroration on the limits of custody but decided his heart wasn't in it. Anyone who could treat his Rosy Posey like that had forfeited the right to mix with decent folk. Let him come back to the place he'd disgraced and live with dirty Gaffer, like a pair of pariahs.

. . .

When they got to Rookery Nook, Robert was surprised to see the bedroom curtains pulled, then alarmed by a flushed and skittish Mother Bear, who had clearly run downstairs to greet the visitors at the back door.

'Oh I wasn't expecting to see you today. Hello, Rose. How's your Father - I mean Mother. Oh, Robert! I wish you'd said you were coming. It's not the best time to call really ... you *should* have said.'

Robert was wrong-footed and asked if she was alright.

She amazed him by blushing and chortling in Rosealea's direction. 'Oh, yes ... it seems I'm a bit of alright.'

Robert gestured to his friend that they should leave but she ignored him and asked Mrs. B what she meant.

'It's your father, Robby, I don't know what's got into him. Went down to the gardens this afternoon to see to his spuds and came back insisting on an early night - well late afternoon more like. He'd seen to his tatties and now it was my turn. He's going to do another hands turn-down there before dark then he'll dig me over again.'

Robert didn't know where to put himself and settled on the back garden, where Rosealea had gone to stifle her hysterics.

'It's not that I'm complaining,' explauned his mother as she followed them. 'Why is Rosy dressed up in that strange costume?'

'Oh I'll tell you another time - something to do with The Sage of Um and the Old Professor.'

'Oh, Rosy dear, if those two are in the same room together, stay well clear.'

Robert heard movement from upstairs and shepherded his colourful companion down the side passage. 'Time we were off, twinkle toes.'

'Where to? You promised cake.'

'To my old man's shed. Let's see what we can find down there.'

The two friends skipped lightly across Bumpy Field to the allotments down by the Gas Works. An abusive Squirrel leered from a gnarled tree to mock Rosealea in her finery. The Squirrel was rebuked by her boyfriend, who told him he knew where they lived.

'Oh, Robert, you really are a wonderful Bear, but that glorified Rat was right. My tutu really is too tight. Help me out.'

> *Will Robert overcome his qualms*
> *To melt in Rosey's rustic charms*
> *With tutu tight and frou-frou bright*
> *She's cast her spell; tonight's the night*
> *Inside the shed with no-one there*
> *Will Rosealea see Robert bare?*

TWO
WHAT A HOOT

WOODVILLE COMMUNITY MENTAL HEALTH
TEAM 9:00 MONDAY 15/5/2017

Willie Mouse says welcome back
There's work to do, no time for slack
Rose the pig says flippin' 'eck
Then Mr. Fox growls, 'watch your step'.

THE TEAM LEADER passed round some minutes from their last meeting. 'Where's Rosealea? She's supposed to be chairing today.'

'Just powdering her snout,' said Robert as he watched her drift past the open window in her balloon of uncertainty.

Then a row broke out in the car park below as she collided with a bicycle ridden by Barry Fox, the area director for social care.

'I was assured you could drive that thing safely; you'll be in breach of your lease at this rate, Miss Piggy.'

'Who are you? Didn't you see me coming?'

Willie Mouse nipped out of the room and down the stairs.

'She must know who Foxy is,' said Ted Sloth, who'd just returned from sick leave.

'Of course she does,' declared Robert, 'she's just being challenging. It'll do for her one day, but you can't say anything.'

The group included two new members: a pair of miniature German Schnauzers called Otto and Lottie, recently qualified, and keen to make good impressions on their first day. They hadn't met Rosealea before and didn't know whether to laugh or put in for transfers.

Ted turned slowly to tell them 'you 'aint heard nothing yet'.

They looked to Robert, who took them through the minutes and ran down the agenda for the day's discussion. Item three concerned the anger-management group.

'Will our Mister Fox be joining us?' asked Lottie.

'Maybes not today, pet,' replied Podgy Pig, the STAR worker who came in late. 'But keep an eye out - you might say his bite's worse than his bark.'

Otto looked at his companion with anxious eyes and drooping whiskers.

Robert wished Podgy would go off sick; no one would miss him, especially his clients.

'You are from the north country, I think,' said Otto, hoping to humanise terrible Podgy. 'The land of the shipyards and the mining of the coal.'

'Aye, that's right, though there's not much of either goes on these days. Now, you're from the land of the converted penalty and ...'

Robert nipped this in the bud. 'Let's run through this now and save time later on, eh?'

Podgy yawned. 'Why not?'

The others showed more interest.

Downstairs, their team leader faced a complex case.

'You'd have seen me coming if you'd looked,' said Rosealea, flaring her nostrils.

Barry Fox was appalled and frowned at Willie Mouse.

'You're team leader here. They seem to come and go as they choose and without heed for the consequences. This lass nearly clattered me - talk about blond bombshells.'

Willie tried to direct attention back to Rosealea and saw that she'd had a striking bleach rinse since he saw her on Friday.

She apologised and expressed what passed for penitence in a flustered pig.

Mr. Fox removed his bicycle clips and tethered his prized Claud Butler 'classic'.

'Why didn't you tell me he was coming, Willie?'

'I did. Why are you so late anyway?'

'Oh, it's been a rough couple of days - you know what we've had on.'

Willie wasn't sure, given it had just been the weekend but let it go as Mr. Fox slunk across the yard. 'Come on then, Mouse, we've wasted enough time. I want to meet your new workers.'

Rosealea gave her manager a funny look. 'I've told you about that too.'

She secured her balloon and trotted crossly up after the others. On her way, she met her chum Tess, the baby elephant, from Older Persons. 'Good weekend, Rosy?'

'Naff off two ton.'

'That's a no then.'

'Oh, I'm sorry, I'll tell you more later - and watch out! Barry Fox is about.'

Robert shunned her windswept mien when Rosealea interrupted the meeting with manager Mouse in full flow. 'It's quite indicative of movement across the care pathways and there are broad implications for change in all our working practice. Barry will tell us more later but first I would like to collate perceptions from within the team;

after all, you will be facing the biggest challenges directly.'

Cobblers thought Robert, but he knew that something was in the air with Foxy sniffing around. He looked around the room. Rosealea had taken a seat next to Podgy, generally a bad sign. Ted was staring at the floor and Barry Fox sat in between Lottie and Otto, who were taking notes as Willie hit his stride, indicatively. He'd got to the proposed changes for Woodville and ballpark estimates.

Ballparks sounded about right to Robert - he tuned out by remembering the Nat 'King' Cole record he played on Saturday as a pissed Rosy dyed - or was it killed? - her hair.

'Care plans roasting on an open fire/ Barry Fox nipping at your ...' He came round just as Willie said, 'Though it's been said many times and many ways, transitions are a given and uncertainty the only fixed point on the public service compass.'

'Nicely put, Will,' said Barry Fox as he turned to the newcomers. 'This is an exciting time to be joining the team. You'll learn a lot here. You've both got mentors?'

'Yes,' replied Willie. 'Otto's with Rosealea and Robert's squiring Lottie.'

This was the first either of the 'seasoned workers' had heard about it, but with Podgy being out of the question and Ted not quite match-fit, it was a buggins' turn for two.

Barry Fox seemed ready to leave but Robert wanted him to stay. He could see that Rosealea might have more to say. If he left, the fur would fly in all directions. 'Can I ask a question?'

'Of course, Robert, I'm here to help.'

'Well, all this stuff about Woodville folk managing their care budgets ... who provides all the care, and what if they spend their money unwisely?'

'You mean, like purchasing a mobile balloon they shouldn't be allowed out with and thereby causing greater needs for social care and consequent demands on finite resources? That sort of thing.'

'Well, no, not that exactly, but ...'

'Or perhaps taking long-term sick leave from your place of work because you've put your carer's allowance in a tip-top high-yield savers account – well, these are the challenges and, as ever, the opportunities. Opportunities to make real differences to the lives of Woodville folk.'

'Any more questions? Good, well, you and I should get together now. Willie, I've got to be back at County Hall for two. Councillor Billy Goat Gruff's been kicking off again about the daft monkeys who've been rehoused on Darwin Street. By the way, is the family known to you at all?'

'What's the name, Barry? We had a few referrals come in last week.'

'Murtagh.'

'That's a Scottish name. Right, if Otto and Lottie can check that with admin, you and I can grab some time, Barry.'

This left the old stagers to collate some perceptions.

> *I've had it now wails Rosealea*
> *My ready tongue will do for me*
> *The news will get to County Hall*
> *I'll wait in dread for Foxy's call.*

'You'll do for all of us, you will, you flap-eared bint,' scoffed Podgy. 'Foxy'll be singeing Willie's whiskers as we speak.'

'Oh, shut it, Pongy. I could slap you, I really could - he's got your number though, hasn't he? You know, they've been auditing the mileage claims?'

Robert couldn't bare this and feared it would give their new chums a bad impression. 'Shut it, the pair of you; what a poor show. Lottie will wonder what she's come to.'

It was a bad thing to say, given his girlfriend's febrile mood and she glared at him. Podgy smirked and made a great play of consulting his diary. There couldn't be much in it, thought Robert.

Lottie returned and asked if anyone had seen 'Herr Mouse'.

'Up the creek,' jeered Podgy as he left the team room.

Rosealea watched him go and ignored the smart little dog who was trying hard to fit in. She had noticed that Robert appeared to be the most sensible of them and took the printed referral details straight to him.

'Hmm,' murmured the capable bear. 'Came in last Thursday via Child Protection. Seems they'd been out earlier, after someone had phoned in with concerns. All they could find was old Granpa Murtagh, who told them the kids were all "at their books" and could they tune his radio into the past. The 1750s, apparently.'

'Will we go straight out? He sounds quite unwell, with ideas of reference.'

'Radio rental, you mean?' asked Rosealea as she eyeballed Robert.

'No, not straight away. Better have a word with the GP, get a bit more background. For all we know, it might be quite normal for him to behave like that - though not in relation to the radio I'd say.'

Rosealea rolled her tiny eyes. 'I'd say you'd better get weaving before there's an incident down Bonkers Street.'

Lottie was not to be quelled. 'It is normal for Scotlanders to reflect on the past, I think - their troubled history and the love they have for a red, red rose.'

That did it. 'You're taking the piss now, Brunhilde, so you better watch it.'

Willie Mouse came back. 'Are you still at it? I've only just buggered Barry back off to County Hall. Honestly, Rose, you do choose your moments.'

'It was windy all of a sudden, I lost control.'

'Oh, well, can't be helped now. Lunch at County Hall should restore him for his meeting with Councillor Bumface. They're a well-matched pair.'

Robert reflected that the day had got off to a bad start. Everyone was cross. He looked at Lottie, who twitched her tail. He handed her the referral and she phoned the Bindweed Surgery to speak to Dr. Slow-Loris.

Rosealea went off to find Otto, as Willie Mouse had suggested she take him along to the Single Point of Access meeting 'to get a feel of the team'. The prospect of a cushy morning mollified the temperamental Tamworth and off she went with something of her old poise.

Willie smiled at Lottie, who favoured him with a full wag this time. 'Well, I'll leave this with you two. Keep me posted.'

Robert took her down to the plaza where a variety of vehicles and bird-powered contraptions waited. He spotted a very flash 'Bustard'-powered Mark 3 and wondered who was flying it.

The large bird was chatting to a local Heron and then Reg Stoat, the chairman of the local health trust, appeared and told it to look sharp. The Heron waved two talons after them.

Robert directed Lottie to his own, more modest set of wings, where he cranked up his trusty little plane and helped Lottie into the passenger seat. As they whizzed down the council runway, he imagined her soft felt ears catching the wind and knew he must touch down as gently as possible.

Before they reached Darwin Street, Robert wanted to make another call - to Loose Tiles, an old farm in the Soggy Mango district, where an Owl has been struggling with anxiety issues. He thought he might do good work with him and also show Lottie what could be done in an integrated team.

As they prepared to land in a lumpy field by the farm, several figures scattered into the untamed woodland.

'Who were they?' asked Lottie after they landed.

'Just a few Romanies. We get them this time of year - no harm in them.'

'You mean, travellers?'

'Yes. Perhaps their caravan is tied up in the forest.'

'Perhaps they would value a social-needs assessment.'

'Perhaps. Let's find Mr. Watson first, he's a funny old bird.'

'He will be up in his tree, yes?'

'Not necessarily, he often visits the farmhouse, according to the farmer. Apparently, he's been doing the odd bit of work for him, and it was the farmer who alerted us. We know him - a bit rough in his ways, but loyal and friendly once he knows you.'

They picked their way to the farmhouse where Robert rapped a rusty knocker. There was no answer even though the door was open.

Lottie looked at Robert with her bright brown eyes and he suddenly felt capable. 'I think we should have a look. Farmer Giles should be about somewhere, and he'll be pleased to see you.'

'Why is that?'

'Well, he's a wire-haired Fox Terrier, very similar to your-self. You may be able to understand him better than I can.'

'You should not assume that we are all alike, Mister Bear. For all you know, I might have more in common with a worm from the garden.'

Oh yeah, thought Mister Bear. 'Well, yes, I see what you mean. Social-care values, embracing diversity. And all that.'

'Yes, I think that is correct.'

Robert was rattled and thought how keen 'Knocker' Giles

would be to embrace diversity once he'd clapped eyes on it. As part of her induction week, it would certainly accelerate the old learning curve. Rosealea was once moved to lay him out with a pitchfork after one encounter - the dirty dog had just lain on his back in a tumescent swoon, saying rough stuff was fine by him. The next time there'd been any business down on the farm, Podgy had been sent.

'Perhaps we should wait a bit, Robert?'

'Fair enough.'

As they toured the grounds, poplars swished in the breeze, which also bore pungent manure their way. A wall-eyed rooster sprinted past with its helmet waggling.

'Perhaps we should go straight in now,' she suggested.

The back door opened directly into the kitchen, where they struggled to make much out. The windows were incredibly dirty but stained light gradually disclosed a grey china sink. Lottie moved closer to Robert as they let their eyes adjust to the gloom.

Working inwards from the window ledge, they saw the rest of what was there: an old table, spattered stove, hardwood chairs, and a big sideboard crammed with pottery, brown envelopes, and more sundry decay from a mouldy farmhouse.

Lottie looked at the dresser and gasped as she saw grubby talons on the top-piece beneath a brown bag of fluff. It moved, causing her to bark, which perturbed the bag as it jumped into the air and disappeared.

'Ah,' said Robert softly. 'That's him. Hello, Mr. Watson, we've come to see how you are.'

There was no answer, then another door banged, and anticipation sharpened the air. 'Hold still, yer thieving Monkeys or I'll blast yer to atoms.'

'It's us, Mr. Giles, Robert Bear - from the social - and a colleague.'

'Oh, well. I'm as well sorting you two public nuisances. Who's your friend? Not that feisty broad you brought before?'

'My name is Lottie, and I am here with Herr Bear. Please lay down your weapon.'

'Oh, very nice, I'm sure.' Then, he rested his gun against the wall and opened some net curtains above the sink.

The visitors could get a better look - of a pile of clothes left on a greasy armchair by the kitchen range and some engine parts stacked together. Then, Lottie saw a rat hopping about near a cupboard. She was on it in a flash and shook the wretched creature till it hung limply from her beard and then she placed it gently by the back door.

Giles looked in wonder. 'I think I'm in love. Come and sit down, eh?'

'No, thank you. I would prefer to stand and, please, let me apologise; it is just bred into my nature. You would prefer to catch your own rats, I'm sure.'

'Hey, any time the fancy takes you - don't mind me.'

Robert had been looking for Mr. Watson and found him perched on top of a door. Giles saw this. 'Oh, it's him you've come for. You can take him with yer; he makes the place look untidy. He's meant to be a creature of the outdoors, not moping in my parlour in the middle of the day.'

Lottie tried to enlighten the rough dog. 'It is possible that your poor Mr. Watson has developed a depressive illness, characterised by prominent anxiety.'

'Well,' said Giles slowly. 'Can you get him right again? You can talk to him in here if you like. I'm off to do some proper work.' He left by the back door and started an old grey tractor.

'What an awful man,' said Lottie. 'Is he normally like that?'

'Call me Bob,' cooed a tired and diminished voice from somewhere above them.

'Come and join us down here,' invited Robert.

'Will she scrag me?' asked Bob.

'We Schnauzers have great respect for the Owl; like us, you are hunters of the first rank.'

'I don't know about that. All I've caught lately are the jitters.' Bob stayed put.

'Come on down,' said Robert. 'I'm sure we can help you.'

'I don't about that. My minds not right - people ask me for wise advice and it comes out daft. I'm scared of field mice. I've been turfed out of my tree by a blasted Pine Martin ...'

'We can help you with re-housing,' advised Lottie.

'Why can't I stop here?'

Robert had an answer for that. 'If you stay here for too long, you could become socially excluded.'

Lottie chimed in, 'One of our mission statements concerns social inclusion and its relevance to good mental health. I am very passionate about this. We are all on a curve.'

'Well, I've been on a rackety curtain rail, so don't expect too many straight lines from me either.'

Lottie appeared put out and asked Robert what he meant. He explained that Bob's thinking was impoverished, he was not himself, what he said could be taken as an index of his melancholy.

Bob heard all this but said nothing as he picked at his ear. She asked him how things had been before his current troubles.

'Ask the Professor; he seems to know more about what's what.'

Robert wondered how the old Prof could fit into the picture, then realised Bob meant him and tried to stop showing off. He explained that Mr. Watson earned his living as a free-lance writer. As 'Wiseacre', he turned out a weekly feature for the *Woodville Bugle* with many a tall tale and droll story. For the past couple of weeks, it had been missing and readers advised that 'Wiseacre is unwell'. Giles found out and contacted social services.

'So, would you let us try to help, Bob?'

'I don't rightly see as how you can.'

Lottie smiled at him. 'Perhaps we could share some amusing stories. In this country, you are fond of the breaking of the wind and the female anatomy. I know many such tales.'

Bob and Robert shared a glance and the Owl asked her if she was having a laugh. Lottie told him she was just trying to help and that it would be better for all if he joined them at their level.

> Mr. Watson joins our team
> And starts again to strut and preen
> Lottie calms his troubled mind
> Such Woodville folk are wise and kind.

Bob puffed up his plumage and looked for a likely roost. He hesitated but Robert told him to 'go for it mate'.

'I can't fly anymore.'

'Poor fellow,' said Lottie sympathetically. 'We can hold this tablecloth out for you.' She pulled at the encrusted material and this seemed to embolden Bob.

He launched up and out into the room, to a post on top of the dresser. He looked a sorry sight with his mangy coat, glassy eye and wayward ears.

'Tell us a good 'un and I'll come down.' Robert cleared his throat but Bob signaled that Lottie should speak.

She asked him why the chicken crossed the road.

'Oh, to get to the other side. That the best you can do?'

'Incorrect Mr. Bob, it was to commit suicide.'

Robert looked through the window as Bob set up a death-rattle wheeze. Its force took him off his perch and he opened his wings to glide beautifully to rest on the sink, avoiding the rising damp and gone-off groceries. Outside, a pig squealed, and a door banged.

'Tell us another Lottie,' requested Bob.

She reeled them off: the farmer's wife and the Billy Goat, the magic trousers of Trieste, and an unlikely story about Johnny Dankworth and the singing Dogs of Darlington. It went down well as Bob had his own amusing tale featuring the genial sax man.

Bob cleared his throat and flapped his wings a bit. Robert reckoned he was looking better.

'Right,' said Bob. 'Johnny and his band are making a record but the studio in Maida Vale is pretty tatty and really needs doing up. The producer apologises but Johnny has a talk with the boys and says they'll decorate if the band gets free studio time. The guy says "yeah man" and they set to work. In no time, it's slapped up a treat and the band starts recording. After-wards, the guitarist says to Johnny "my fingers had paint on them while I was blowing" and, quick as a flash, Johnny says, "I've never heard you play with so much emulsion before".'

Lottie laughed out loud, but Robert only got half the story as he'd paid more attention to the roughhouse in the yard. Giles was getting the worst of a ruck, with a stubborn pig who seemed disinclined to leave the comfort of his little house. 'Will that go into your next column Bob?'

'I'm not sure, it's been a couple of weeks now, and I'd been recycling some thin stuff. I'd like to use some of yours Lottie - you'd get full credit.'

'No, no, but perhaps we can get together and consider some CBT for your anxiety, yes?'

'Couldn't you tell me some more jokes?'

Robert thought it might come down to the same thing, but he couldn't deny the form Lottie had shown so far. She certainly had a way with melancholic Owls, a developing group according to the Old Professor, who had been tasked by the Health Trust to research this, now that he was well again, following that unfortunate business with that dodgy jam. He felt it was time he called round for tea with Woodvilles resident boffin, who had been a mentor to the bear over the years. He'd stay off any food on offer though.

'How do you get on with Farmer Giles Bob? Is it right you do some work for him?'

'He's better for knowing, certainly. How I got to be here tells you a lot about my difficulties, I suppose.'

Lottie encouraged him and he gave her a palsied hoot. 'It's interesting alright. It begins one night when my dad and his mate were out looking for some prey - anything really. They're both hopeless hunters but you can't say anything. Anyway, we hadn't eaten for days. Vic's lot had kicked him out so he came round and that was another beak to fill, so they thought they'd fly here for some easy pickings ... I mean, you can see what it's like - Liberty Hall, winders wide open at all hours and many a tasty morsel to make off with. Well, they've caught nowt in the yard and park themselves on the sash looking in. Vic sees something twitch by a chair, so they go for it; is it a rat, a fat mouse, maybe a dying squirrel? No, it turns out to be Farmer Giles' tail, obscured by the mucky sacking he's covered himself with. He comes round in a flash, clouts the pair of them, then bags them up in a potato carrier.'

'Very strong, those potato bags,' attested Robert.

'But did they get away?' asked Lottie.

Bob chuckled again. 'He let them go after they'd been made to sing for their supper.'

Robert was interested by now and asked Bob what 'the crack' was.

'Giles is a great man for the opera and is, in fact, an accomplished singing dog himself. He parks our two on the dresser and commissions them to cry up a selection from *The Flying Dutchman.*'

'Ah yes,' said Lottie. 'A wonderful lieder - and they were familiar with it?'

'Well, whatever it was they came up with, went down well enough. Anyway, once Giles had thrown back his head and joined in, it didn't seem to matter. Dad said he was quite good actually. After a while, he finds them a dead rat each and tells them to call in any time they're passing.'

Robert saw the lieder-loving terrier outside, looking the worse for his tussle with the pig. On his way to the farmhouse, he was diverted by two ducks who seemed keen to tell him something. One of them pointed its wing and he followed them towards the Old Mill Stream.

'So why did you get involved in this, Bob?'

'Naturally, those two didn't fancy a return engagement at the Woodville Opera House but felt that Farmer Giles and I would get on just fine and, therefore, for the good of the family and soft Uncle Vic, I should make myself known round here and sing for their suppers. I says "yeah alright" ... and that was six weeks ago. I've been unable to get out for the last two. Dad comes to fetch "the catch" and tells me I'll get used to it; he'll see to my writing for me. I haven't seen him for a week and this great woe has come upon me like that bloke in the desert. What was his name?'

'Job,' said Lottie.

'What?' asked Bob.

'It was Job, Bob,' replied Robert.

'Was it a good job? Must have been doing better than me,' said Bob, who began to weep at the recollection of his family's abandonment.

The pathos was palpable. Lottie was moved to touch his

talons and reaffirm that they would do all they could to help and that the organisation they represented had many rooms for the sick at heart.

Robert couldn't believe what he was hearing but had an idea of his own. 'Will you talk some more to Lottie while I find Farmer Giles?'

Bob agreed and Robert stepped into the yard.

From one of the stained outbuildings, a dank looking Cow gave him a rheumy eye as he passed. His Doc Martens got stained. Everywhere there was mud and worse.

'Over here,' called the farmer. He was busy in the small meadow, doing something to a stone wall. Several Ducks sat at a distance, watching him work. 'You're a helpful sort, Robert, come and lend a hand, eh,' asked a wheezy Giles.

The Ducks cackled and Robert got to think that farm labour was fine work for a man but also that his own good works were not dissimilar, sometimes being called to help repair walls of an inner world. When they'd finished the drystone wall, they caught a brief sunburst, and Giles moved his tail. He thanked the Ducks for alerting him and they waddled off happily to their work.

'Right, lad, I reckon me and thee's earned a cup of tea.'

Robert gave a gruff 'aye', then brought up the Bob question.

'Well, Robby, has he told you about his father and friend? Right pair of Herberts but could pipe it up like little larks, so I thought it would suit all. I'd have some fun and they could make their marks up back at home. I was a bit disappointed when they sent the lad along but he's a beautiful voice too, so I didn't bother. Then he started hanging about the house all day and when he burst into tears during an evening of *South Pacific,* I knew it wasn't right.'

'What song were you doing?'

'"Happy Talk".'

'Ah, that would be the irony, eh?'

'Don't start talking daft to me, Robert. Reckon you can get him right?'

'Has he said much to you about what's bothering him?'

'Not a lot. You'd think one of his lot would have been round by now. Are they not bothered, he's such a canny lad?'

Robert could see that Giles had grown fond of Bob and wondered if a short-term payment of carer's allowance would help pave the way forward. The farmer took umbrage at this. 'It's a bad thing when we have to be paid to look out for one another. Still, keeps your lot in work, I suppose.'

Robert moved the talk to farming business and the 'plutocracy from Brussels'.

Giles gave him another funny look. 'They're right enough'.

The Pig who'd given him trouble earlier trundled across their path. Giles kicked 'the fat bastard'.

Robert wondered if he ever grew attached to his stock.

'You must be joking - I've plans for that one.'

Robert reminded himself that Ted Giles was a north countryman and that his coarse manner cloaked a gruff warmth. As they neared the farmhouse, the back of Bob's head could be seen be seen nodding attentively through the mucky windowpane. They went in. Bob looked directly at Giles and said 'hello'.

'Come on,' said Lottie to Robert. 'I want to see the farm.'

> Lottie speaks of Bob's distress
> His life's gone wrong, it's all a mess
> His family dynamics are up the spout
> No one loves you when you're down and out.

Robert closed the back door upon hearing the sound of soft laughter from the farmer to a quip from Bob. Lottie picked her way over to the tractor shed and gestured that she and Robert should go inside.

Once there, she asked if she could sit on the tractor and he helped her up. He noticed her long bandy back legs and lovely hairy chest but felt guilty. He and Rosealea had been doing each other's heads in recently and her bleary unconcern earlier had left him shocked. He couldn't think what had gotten into her. Lottie looked happy handling the steering wheel and making 'brrm-brrm' noises.

It took an effort to get back to the business of Bob. 'So, what did he say then?'

'He disclosed emotional abuse, financial exploitation, and the shocking treatment of an elderly Tawny Owl. Bob's father and uncle are shameless wasters who take the "old granny's" benefits, bully his mother, and leave Bob and the younger ones to fend for themselves. Also, they mock Bob's talent but pocket his fees.'

'There's a safeguarding issue there, at the very least. This is a different story to *Tales from The Vienna Woods*.'

'Yes, the mice-catching was only partly true, and Giles is cross at being so easily tricked. He believes in Bob, though ... but he is very wary of telling his tale, in case it makes things worse for his granny. The last he heard, she had been pushed out onto a narrow branch and threatened with being brought out of retirement.'

Robert looked thoughtful, then began to outline one of his favourite themes: how life experience and stress vulnerability factors are implicit determinants in individual depression.

Lottie cut him short. 'What shall we do now, though?'

Robert thought some more. 'Go back to the office and hold an outline case review.'

Lottie had begun to see that Robert was a twit. 'There should be steps we can take here, now, *today*.'

'Yes, has it stopped raining out there?'

'Have a look.'

Robert stuck his nose outside but decided it didn't matter. 'It's alright.'

Lottie stayed on the tractor, so he leaned against the door. 'What do you think then?'

She rested her chin on the steering wheel and looked into the middle distance. 'We must find alternative housing for Bob, fix him up with direct payments, provide supportive counselling and coordinate effective monitoring of his recovery. Help me down, please.'

'Right, well, that's us done here then.'

As they made their way back to the house, Robert asked Lottie how she would take it on. 'You could make an appointment to see Bob again soon and start it rolling, and I will make sure this is alright with the gentleman farmer.'

Robert arranged to see Bob in two days' time. As he left the kitchen, the Owl was back up on the dresser whistling, 'A House Is Not A Home'. He found his colleague down by the Old Mill Stream, giving up a merry chuckle to something Farmer Giles was telling her. She joined him and they walked over to his plane.

Robert reckoned it had not been a bad morning's work, all things considered, and he already had an idea about Bob's new beginning.

As they glided away, through sun-brushed vapours, Lottie asked Robert about the other task they were supposed to take on. He told her not to worry as he'd commissioned a little Owl to take a message back to 'HQ', explaining their situation. Manager Mouse would have sorted something out. Nevertheless, he took them on a longer route back and showed Lottie more of Greater Woodville; she enjoyed views of the Mukee-Heron Industrial Estate, set by the River Slither.

Then he pointed out the floodlight pylons at Wood Head Park, the home of Woodville Town. Lottie shouted that she loved football and Robert felt a flash of complex emotions. As they descended to bypass a cherubs' conference on cloud nine, Robert took them over a building site which he later told her was the 'Clean Slate' project, run by the Acorn Trust, where Bob might start his new life.

As she hopped up the steps to the office, Robert felt more of the troubling affect he noticed in the air when she said she liked football.

> *Robert's boss is not impressed*
> *He'll give the wrong impression to their guest*
> *The manager's temper is torn and frayed*
> *His day has seen another trust betrayed.*

As he walked down the corridor to the team room, Robert heard Salome, a sleek Harris Hawk, who was one of the CPNs, asking if 'Piggy Pig' had returned.

Willie Mouse told her he had but was currently seeing what was cracking off with a gang of chimps that Mr. Bear was meant to be dealing with. Robert made way for Salome as she hopped out of the office and saw that Lottie was writing in a smart notebook.

Willie caught his eye and nodded towards his own little office. Once there, the atmosphere changed, and Robert found himself on the wrong end of a bollocking.

'Fart arseing about down on the farm, pleasing yourself, subjecting Lottie to that dirty dog - depressed Owls, you're taking the pee, you are.'

'Lottie accustomed herself very well. It's quite a complex case. You know, if—'

'Don't talk to me like that, you silver-tongued twat.'

Robert got a handle on his precious tongue and reflected that his manager might well have one on him, given the day he'd had. After more bluff reflections from Willie, he got a chance to tell his side of things as both of them stood looking neutrally out the window.

An Anteater in a velocipede glided above a large chestnut tree and encountered difficulties as a smaller craft, fashioned from a large, upturned umbrella, darted about it. A monkey's hand could be seen lobbing objects at the larger craft. The Anteater's superior pedal power took it out of harm's way as other monkeys leapt to a tree branch.

'I blame that Cheruby Clarkson,' said Willie with a sigh. 'Go on, I'm listening.'

Robert continued their debrief, emphasising Lottie's good work, the value of financial support to farmer Giles ('you *are* joking') and the good offices of the Acorn Trust. 'Best have a word with Tom Tit then, Robert - see if there are any vacancies.'

'Will do, but what about these Monkeys?'

'What about them?'

'Well, I know Youth Treatment schemes fell out of favour a while ago, but we should be proposing some kind of community-based type stuff.'

'Have a word with your new friends down on yonder farm.'

Willie laughed as he left the room, but his comments set Robert thinking.

> *A full day's work and new chums too*
> *Robert thinks there's lots to do*
> *He knows that Rosy waits at home*
> *But he longs increasingly for time alone*
> *Their love has passed through many changes*
> *Now he wanders through his own back pages.*

THREE
COME FLY WITH ME

The daily grind can be too much
Our love-stuck chums don't like the rush
And packing for hols, can bring on stress
Have you filled the car up, ironed my dress?

'IT'S HERE behind the door, where you left it. Look.'

'Oh. Well, why didn't you tell me? You knew I was going to wear it today.'

No, he didn't. And why the sudden interest in all this girly gear; Robert thought of Rosealea as a modern kind of girl. In trousers. He'd noticed her packing a copy of *Bridget Duck's Diary* for her holiday reading, where before she might have taken a feministic novel by Stig Spoonbill. He'd heard that you never begin to know someone until you've been on vacation with them. They should have a better idea of the shape of things to come after their week at Redcar.

. . .

She had kicked up to begin with when he told her. It was up north, wasn't it, where people were rough? He told her the beaches were grand and there was plenty to do, and under the circumstances, it was the best he could manage. After all, Willie Mouse had been good to give them time off at short notice. If it hadn't been for Ted coming back, and Otto and Lottie settling in ....

'Can you give me a hand with these bags. I've got bad guts again.'

'Yeah, I'll put them in the plane.'

When he opened up the space beneath the fuselage, Robert saw he'd need to repack in order to get it all in. With Rosy's guidance, he managed to stow their luggage and had time to plan the flight path while she had a last look round. He penciled in a touchdown at York to break the journey. He could show Rosealea the permanent exhibition of 'Pigs in Muck' at the Tang Hall Sculpture Park, a favourite of his from childhood trips to Granpa Bear's house in Dringhouses.

When Rosealea appeared, locking the front door behind her, Robert saw how tired she looked. He'd try his best to make their week special. He'd learned some more about her difficult life.

She'd never known, for sure, who her real father was, and her mother had abandoned the family for long stretches of her childhood, which was lived on a remote smallholding. In the end, she'd been fostered with the Weasels on Startrite Road, who'd discovered she was bright and had sorted out her education.

Robert was only her third 'proper boyfriend'. She climbed up to the passenger's seat, allowing him to watch her through a mirror. The wind brushed her bristles, and the darting sun caught her snout, making it glisten. He thought she was very beautiful just then and was shamed by his glances in Lottie's direction. Compared to Rosealea, she was just a dog.

'Off we go then, Captain Bear,' she called.

This was more like the girl he'd been used to. He opened his throttle and charged down the field to lift them off, off and away. He did a circle of the land below them.

Woodville folk were dawdling ants, the woods sprigs of broccoli. They soon passed over the Old Professor's castle, where a tiny arm waved from a turret. Robert identified Trevor, the Prof's laboratory assistant, who'd had a difficult time of it when his boss went bonkers for a while.

Robert reflected on a job well done, all happily mended. No doubt, Trevor was signaling this back to him.

Down below, Trevor Morris was thinking it had been a long shot and wondering how much longer the doors behind him would hold.

'Did you see him?' Robert shouted.

'See who?'

'Trevor, the Professor's minion?'

'No, that place gives me the willies anyway.'

Robert nodded without really hearing and concentrated on climbing as he took them beyond Nutbush City limits and the county borders. After half an hour or so, the mighty Humber Bridge came into view below thinning clouds. This told Robert they were not far from York and he soon brought them down in a field by a river.

The landing upset Rosealea and she chucked up behind a bush. A passing badger asked if 't'lass is right' in a way which puzzled Robert. He'd forgotten that people in the north were so direct.

After some blokey banter, 'Timmy' advised Robert about parking 'Firefly', then wandered off toward the town.

'Finished with your new chum then?'

'Eh, oh I'll just get the plane over by those trees, then we'll go up to York.' She gave him a blank look and went to gaze at the river.

Robert was aware that his beloved had lost her sparkle and knew he should say something as soon as he'd secured their stuff. 'You seem a bit off it Rosy – your, er, petals have a muted hue.'

But her thorns hadn't lost their edge. 'You've noticed, have you? Percy Throwup.'

'Yes, well you've been sick too, haven't you?'

She gave him her flat look and suggested a walk into town might help, though not to the stupid display he mentioned. Betty's Café would be more like it. She put a trotter through his arm, and they made a seemly walk along the river side. Happy families crowded the cool compartments of passing cruisers and scavenging seagulls fought for bread cast by laughing children. Rosy remarked that York was a nicer spot than Woodville and wouldn't it be good to try for jobs here?

'You mean, move away? Leave Woodville?'

'Yeah. What do you think?'

Robert noticed a sporting clubhouse over the river and drew her attention to it. 'Hey, look at that.'

'What?'

'Them rats over there, getting that long boat out of the shed.'

'Is there a point to this, Robert?'

'There'll be a race soon - bound to be.'

She gave him another look, but he'd bought some time. Then a brown Rat on a bike shot past, causing Rosealea to gasp in alarm.

'Be careful!' called Robert.

'Bog off,' shouted the Rat.

'Young tearaway,' muttered Robert. 'Probably from a dysfunctional hole.'

'Come on, we're on holiday - where's this café?'

> *A table for two shows a tempting spread*
> *But Rosealea gets a pain in the head*
> *Then worse to come, some startling news*
> *On which our pair hold differing views.*

As they climbed from the riverbank to join the throng, Robert became protective and held Rosealea closer. There were many tall buildings, and he spied the cathedral's towers further off in the town. Vehicles moved slowly, close to the busy footpaths. It reminded him of a book he knew by Boris Barmicus, or 'the Bearded Tit' as he was better known, where loveless trolleybuses rattled down cobbled streets. The hero had been knocked about by life and his dreams lay broken on the road as the woman he loved signaled poignantly from the back of a bus. Their paths never did connect, and it was all very sad.

He pictured a bereft Rosy staring tearstained from the window of a Woodville single decker. That must never happen to them. Leaving Woodville might begin a process of separation that would tear their love apart. He'd read about that too. It would be a moment of bifurcation and he would tell her this when the time was right.

·   ·   ·

The shiny frontage of Bettys famous café appeared across a busy square. 'What do you think, Rosy? Wait till you see their custard fancies.'

'There's a queue.'

Two Pelicans at the back wobbled forward. 'Be worth it, it's moving.'

'Okay, but do you mind standing here? I've just got to nip for something.'

Before he could say anything, she was off, down the main street and soon lost in the crowd. It was Boris Beardie again. And wasn't there a poem about a fellow struggling for breath while next door another one blew his nose? 'Are you going in or what?' A voice from further north, song-like and insistent.

He went in to stand behind the pelicans. Behind him, Gateshead wit pranced forth. 'Them two'll tek some filling eh, pair of sticky beaks, I'll bet there's fish pie on the menu.'

The older Bird looked round. Sensing trouble, Robert told him that there should be some very nice-scented teas available. The Pelican nodded blandly and turned away. Robert overheard a quieter remark about 'haddock scented like' and saw in the window's reflection that the cheeky customers were a pair of dowdy water voles. Then he saw Rosealea come into the café.

She bustled upstairs, carrying a paper bag. Then the Pelicans were taken through to be seated by the Smooth Fox Terrier in charge. He soon turned back to Robert and asked him if 'it is just for one sir?'

He explained that his companion wouldn't be long and was shown to a table. He saw that the voles were behaving themselves since they'd clapped eyes on the head waiter.

The waitress was hovering, so he ordered for them. A nice

big macaroon washed down by orange pekoe would see her right, then a few good walks when they reached the coast.

He'd just taken his first sip when she joined him. She looked worse than ever and had been crying. 'Rosy, what is it?'

'I can't face anything, Robert. Let's get out of here.'

As they got up to go, one of the voles asked if they could have their cakes. Robert said yes but told the chief on the way out that his 'friends from the north' would be paying.

'Let's go somewhere quiet,' said Rosealea.

So, he took her to the tomb of Saint Tibullus, where she told him she was pregnant.

'Pregnant?'

'Yeah.'

Robert looked at the stained plaque telling of the 13-century cat martyred for putting it about that Jesus came from Darlington. Heresy of the worst kind. 'I'll stand by you, pet; it could all be for the best, meant to be even ...'

'I've decided what I'm going to do.'

'Yes right - what?'

'I don't want this baby.' She looked at the stony sarcophagus and wondered at the folly of animal kind. Why couldn't they be more like saps, blameless and unthinking, content to shuffle through life, just taking what came? That medieval moggy should have kept his daft ideas to himself - it would have to have been a 'he'. Earlier, Robert had shown her a statue of Harold Hare, the railway king who'd disgraced himself by embezzling funds. She asked him why he'd put his fingers in the till.

'I'd say a combination of the temptations of unfettered capital, the amorality of extended paternalism, the growth of towns, and being a fast runner.'

Rosealea laughed, so he asked her how far gone she was.

'I'm two weeks overdue, so I bought some testing powders

while you queued and did the business in Betty's bogs. I'm sorry but I just didn't fancy that macaroon; it was very thoughtful of you.'

'Are these powders reliable; they don't have anything to do with the Old Professor?'

'I shouldn't think so and they are reliable, especially for we Pigs. Besides, I'm pretty sure when I caught on.'

'Well why didn't you say so - if you knew?'

'Because you can be wrong, twit face.'

Robert was stung by this. 'When was it then?'

'That night there was nowt on telly, and you came and went without signing you're name in the visitors' book.'

He wished he'd said nothing. 'All very romantic, I'm sure.'

'Well, it's left us in a not very romantic situation.'

Robert thought about Harold Hare. He must have left a few visitors' books unsigned; these things happened to a chap. 'Shall we press on to Redcar? Shame to miss the seaside.'

'Oh ... yeah, I was just worried about telling you. Come on, Tiger, fly me to the moon.'

This was said without much conviction, but Robert appreciated the gesture and tried not to treat her like a wilting bloom. They sat down by a railway bridge on the way to watch the rowers. A sharp prow appeared from beneath the bridge and seemed to rest before delayed power forced it forward.

Rosealea chuckled as a crew of Ferrets emerged and caught the afternoon sun. The cox-bawling encouragement was a Field Mouse. 'Faster, you set of tarts.'

The next crew was a group of brindled Guinea Pigs, coxed by a gobby Blue Tit, who shouted that they didn't want to get beaten by 't' scruffy buggers'.

'They're very competitive, aren't they, Robby?'

'Got to be, really. Do you remember when Willie Mouse organised a five-a-side against Forest Town Probation? Told us it was just a bit of fun and to go out and enjoy ourselves. They had a rookie in, who'd played for Nutbush reserves. Kicked us off Sweetbriar rec. Then told us we didn't try hard enough ... how it was an insult to turn up like big blouses. I learned something that night.'

'Oh, yeah?'

'Put yourself into things fully. Treat the visitor's book like a novel with many chapters, not a notebook of quick sketches. I also found out that Teddy Bear from over their way has a strange tattoo on his bottom.'

Rosealea showed some interest. 'What is it?'

'One of the others saw me looking, so I left it.'

'They already think you're an item of women's clothing.'

'Not me personally. I played well; you ask Ted.'

'Yes, alright, Rodney Marshwarbler, can we get off now? I feel well enough to fly again.'

> *The clouds were like an alabaster palace*
> *As Robert took Firefly through the sky*
> *Her nose shone like a red and ruby chalice*
> *As Rosealea guessed where their future*
> *   might lie.*

The take-off from York had been bumpy, leaving Rosealea crumpled in the back. Robert saw this as he glanced in his mirror and decided to take them out to sea, where it was calmer. It started to rain, so Rosealea tied her bonnet tighter and shouted at the pilot, 'Robby isn't there a magic island somewhere out here?'

He hadn't a clue what she was on about but said 'probably', thinking she must be getting confused with Puff the Magic

Dragon, who lived near Peterlee and often helped the local police with their enquiries. He pointed out Hartlepool docks as they came inland.

The guesthouse, Dabbers Rest, had a Woodville connection. The owner was Kev Rat and his brother, Dave, ran the Wizbang Garage on the industrial estate. He'd serviced Firefly recently and put Robert onto 'our kids hotel'. Robert made the reservations that night. As they descended, Rosealea became queasy and boaked demurely over the side.

Some passing Seagulls took an interest, which made her feel much worse. By the time he took them down on the beach, she was fed up with their little adventure and asked Robert to take her back to Woodville as soon as she was better. 'Talk about turbulence, I'm just glad I passed on that sticky bun at York. Here, give me a hand, you great wazzock.'

Robert asked after her hormones and she slapped him on the head. 'I believe that's how they do things up here,' she said. Then the fight went out of her and she put herself meekly into his forgiving arms.

'Right,' he said. 'The plane'll be fine here for the time being and it's just a short walk to the top, so we'll settle in and have a nice rest then ...'

'I'll have a lie down. You can find out about all those nice things to do. You mentioned supernatural phenomena. I could do with some of that.'

When they got to the steps with the bags, he saw it would be a two-stage operation. Then a friendly Octopus turned up and went into its dance of greeting. This amused Rosy, so he offered to help with the bags. In no time at all, the holidaymakers were within sight of their guesthouse.

'Oh, Robby, I've never seen anything so funny. I think I'm going to like Redcar after all.'

Robert was glad she'd been able to sample some of the local warmth he'd been prattling about. He lugged the bags down towards a row of detached houses with sea views. Ratty's place was bound to be there.

The houses had names like Bella Vista, Whoopers, and Bide-A-Wee, but by the time they got to Dabbers Rest, it was the end of the line leading to a lost looking space, where rubbish and old cement gathered. The nearest dwellings were stuck on a long and dingy looking road, leading away from the front. It was called Top Street and Robert led Rosealea across it. The next place was the edge of a windy golf course, where a smart looking weasel in a cap was moving a golf ball with his foot. He seemed edgy but relaxed when he saw that they were lost and gave them directions.

'It's on Top Street, Rosy. That place we just passed. I'm sure it'll be very nice inside.'

When they got halfway down the street, Robert crossed over to avoid some rundown buildings. Their place had to be on the other side of the street, but a local resident sent them back, and he heard someone say 'fuck off' from the house with a broken window, which was Dabbers, apparently.

Rosealea knocked on the door and another voice from inside said 'you lying get'. She stood back to look up to the first floor. There was a small face squinting back from a mildewed window. A mole in a baseball cap smiled hopefully at Rosealea;

then the face disappeared and the front door was opened by another, older, mole in painter's overalls. 'Who are you like?' he demanded.

'Is Kev - Mr. Rat in?' asked Robert.

'I never smashed yon winder,' said the younger Mole.

'Shut yer gob, man; they've not come about that,' said his mate, nodding at the bags. 'You'd best come round the back, Ratty's down the bookies again, soft bugger.'

Robert tried to be friendly. 'He's a betting man then?'

'Oh, aye. He wanted to bet us you'd not turn up. He's bet us we won't finish the job by tea-time.'

'Well, he's right there,' said the other one (Ralph), who was turned on by the bigger mole (Derek).

'I've told you, ya little twat. If it wasn't for our lass, I'd have nowt to do with yer.'

Rosealea asked him quietly if this was an example of northern warmth and wit. Robert asked Ralph if their room was ready.

'Is that the one we did first, Unc?'

'Aye, go on - show them up, Einstein.'

The house was big and dark. In fact, as far as Robert could see, there were no lights at all. He told Rosealea that, historically, regional moles made excellent decorators as their large and floppy hands make them adept at slapping up paint and wallpaper. However, they had to work in the dark to get their best results.

'Anyone else on the job then?' asked Rosealea. 'A team of bats?'

Robert gave the lad a pound and told him they'd be fine. Rosealea was soon snoring, and he began to ache with tenderness for her as he sat in a nice wicker chair by the window.

They were going to have a baby but what kind of baby? He knew there were some examples of love taking a hand where nature was uncertain. Perhaps it was all for the best.

From his seat by the window, he could see the backyard where a motorbike leaned against the rough wall and random rubbish twitched in the wind. Beyond the yard, the landscape opened out; there was a small children's playground looking a bit lost in unruly grass. After the seesaw and swings, the land stretched over to the backs of the nicer houses, then a gap, where Robert could see the sea and sky. This was one of his favourite views, a free space where the elements met and moved through changing light and nothing much mattered. Nothing really mattered at all as Freddie Meerkat had sung.

He started to hum, then remembered Rosy, and looked back at the play area where an old Bear was swinging a smaller one around.

Robert's leg was in an awkward position, tucked under the chair, and his reverie petered out when he shifted some weight. This generated a pleasant rustling but also a louder crack as one of the legs gave way.

Rosealea stirred. 'Gnrr, bleurgh. What was that?'

'This chair's bad, so don't sit in it.'

'What, you mean in my condition?'

Robert moved across to the bed and she made space for him. The day was fading slowly, and without lights the room took on the air of a small boudoir in a long Venetian afternoon ... the gondoliers smoking by the water, the evening full of promise.

Rosealea sensed his gay holiday mood. 'You really like it here, don't you?'

'Yeah, it's okay. What do you think?'

'Well I don't suppose we've seen the best of it yet.'

'Shall we have a walk in a bit, maybe a drink?'

'Why not?'

He decided to share his reflections from the free space, where nothing mattered, and told her that perfect moments took the sting out of the other stuff.

Rosealea thoughts were more earthbound. 'Robert, what do you reckon to this baby - *our* baby? Was it a bright moment when I told you?'

'No, it was a shock ...'

'I bet. How do you think I felt?'

He looked at the ceiling but there were no epiphanies there, just polystyrene and eavesdropping Spiders. 'How did you feel though?'

'It reminds me of the time I thought I'd caught on with Peter Rabbit - should have seen him run that day.'

Robert was aghast. 'Peter Rabbit ... Peter Pissypants Rabbit. I never knew you'd been out with him.'

'It was ages ago. Courting strong at one time we were though. I thought you knew.'

The things women thought you knew - try getting anything to settle in their vaporous and variegated noddles. The bucktoothed numpty. 'Courting strong, what a charming expression.' Robert was rattled. 'So, what happened then, with Peter?'

'Oh, I came on late but he'd muckied his ticket by then, all for the best, I suppose. He was well in with the Barkers you know. Ruined him really.'

'Hey, I saw Sue Barker the other day.'

'No, where?'

'Down the cop shop, what a sight - she'd had her tail bleached and a ring in her nose. You know, her lot account for a lot of the petty crime in Woodville and they breed like stink.'

'Yes, well, as I say, I'm glad I didn't.'

Robert pulled her closer and told her that he respected Rabbits because they were grounded, closer to the earth, and went their own way.

'Oh, Robert, you're a wonderful bear. I love to hear you talk. It's generally bobbins but I don't care. Tell us another.'

Robert hesitated and moved his paw into a more comfortable position on Rosealea's belly. 'Okay. I knew this old rabbit once, Mr. Backhouse; he was an old mate of R.D. Lamb.'

'Who?'

'You know, the radical psychiatrist; anyway, old Bob Backhouse had been trying for years to work out something Lamby had said to him. He said, "if I don't know I don't know, I think I know, if I didn't know I know I know, I think I don't know".'

'Right, what the chuff does that mean?'

'I don't rightly know, I think.'

'You're having a laugh and I reckon K.D. Lamb was as well.'

'R.D. For Ronnie. Very influential in his day.'

'If that's radical psycho-talk, our dad was at it as well; some of the stuff he came out with on Sunday afternoons. I could do with a drink right now. Are you up for this walk?'

Robert thought he would sooner lie where he was with his best girl by his side, watching the stars come out. 'Yes, alright. I'd better see if Kev Rat's back before we go though.'

The lights were back on downstairs. The smell of paint was pungent, and music was playing at the back of the house. It was Piggy Pop singing, 'Never Met a Girl like You Before'. He went towards the sound of the grizzled warbler and gave out a polite 'hello'.

'Who's that like'?

'Robert Bear and chum. Your friends let us in.'

The door opened. 'They's no friends of mine - idle and slapdash. Look at that dado - I'm expecting you, am I?'

'Yes, your brother fixed it up, he's another chum of mine.'

'Our kid - aye, it's all coming back. You'll be Soft Walter. What do you think of your room? Disgraceful isn't it.'

'What's Ratty like then?' asked Rosealea.

'Aging rocker in a green cardie. Do you know what his brother the grease monkey calls me?'

'Tell me while we walk into town. I want to see the war memorial and the pavilion, then perhaps have a sherry before bed.'

'I think there might be a sherry on offer somewhere.'

To reach Greater Redcar, they needed to go down to a small harbor, lit up beautifully by round lights. The tide was coming in and they could hear the sea launching itself against the pebbles.

'Isn't there a poem about that?' asked Robert. 'One of those Victorian jobs about life and God?'

'Yes, sweetheart, there generally is.'

Robert remembered the pebble-dashed poet. What should he do? He spotted a green metal bench further down and led her to it. 'It was Mathew Aardvark; he was a school inspector. Should we call our baby Redcar, or maybe Saltburn - Salty for short - or Red?'

'Our mam was right about you. How on Earth did I get into this?'

'Well, I think there's been an element of consent ...'

'Shut up, clever arse. So, you've been thinking about things, in your own little way and decided the patter of tiny trotters, paws, or God knows what might be fun?'

Robert remembered an assertion-skills workshop he'd been

advised to go on. 'Certainly. I want us to start a family, our family. It's our time.'

'Is that right, Pa? What was it we were going to call it: South Shields?'

'It depends on whether it's a boy or girl.'

'Or mongrel outcome ... not otherwise specified.'

'Ah, now, I've been looking into that?'

'When?'

'Let's go for a drink and I'll explain.'

> *A cheering drink a canny chat*
> *There's nowt can go much wrong with that*
> *But John Barleycorn comes to play his part*
> *And Robert ends up broken on a coal man's*
>   *cart.*

The nearest 'boozer', as Robert understood pubs in Redcar to be called, was just by the harbour. The Fishers Arms bore a sign creaking rhythmically in the sea breeze, bearing a mighty Elephant swinging a bulging net of happy fish. The landlord was actually a small Elephant and showed them into a sparse tap room.

Two pints later, Rosealea had reached a mood of settled jollity. 'You're right, Robby, it *is* friendly up here.'

Then a fight broke out in the lounge between a pair of old-aged Pelicans. A tankard flew through, into the tap, and the landlord ejected the dowdy birds, advising them to settle their differences 'out the back'.

'I know what you mean, Rosy - they're more open with their feelings. Fancy another?'

'Why not? And some soggies, eh?'

Rosealea looked around the room as he gave their orders. The adjacent table was taken by a pair of Badgers sharing a bottle of Merlot. Then a Rooster in leathers pranced in, followed by some other bikers, then an Owl and a Pussycat, two Otters and a swarthy Mouse with his helmet still on.

Robert came back and suggested they hang on to their seats as the place was filling up, so they might hear the singer who was due on later. The mouse, called Ian, came over to their table with one of the otters and asked if the empty seats were taken.

'No, they're free,' answered Rosealea and moved her handbag.

The mouse sat next to her and took off his helmet. This confused Rosealea because from the shoulders up he was a marmoset monkey. Robert had done plenty of diversity aware-ness training and took it in his stride, but Rosealea couldn't take her eyes off him. She found her tongue at last. 'Where did you get that lovely skid lid?'

'Feller in Stockton - Pikes Bikes.'

Robert asked him if he'd come to hear the singer before Rosy could ask where he got his head from. 'Aye, brilliant, but not from Stockton.'

Ian's mate started moaning about the beer, so Rosealea and Robert moved into a huddle in the corner. He told her about his chat with the landlord, partly to stop her gawping at Ian. 'While he was pulling the pints, he gave me an account of how the human mind works ...'

'How do you reckon Ian's mind works?'

'Never mind that, listen ... it involves two great truths that must be understood. Firstly, that the mind is divided into parts, which sometimes conflict and, like a rider on an elephant, the conscious, reasoning part of the mind has only limited control over what the beast does. The second truth is that our life is the creation of our mind. The Buddha said that.'

Rosealea sipped her Strongarm ale and said that the Buddha must have come from Stockton.

'I suppose it's possible,' said Robert. 'If Jesus came from Spennymoor, or wherever it was.'

'Move up, pet,' said a pissed Squirrel as the place took in more music lovers.

By the time the band arrived, the holidaymakers were wedged in tight by the fireplace, and Rosealea was dying for a pee. Robert advised her to go while the going was good.

While she was away, he made a discreet study of Ian and his companions, who all seemed happy enough to drink with him. The landlord's ideas set him thinking. If your life was the construction of your mind, all you had to do was have a good think and things would work out. Robert knew he was well oiled, but wasn't that when your mind was most fluid and your best ideas came along, like a compliant Elephant? Rosealea returned and he gave her some money before she could sit down. 'Get 'em in, pet, and have a word with Epi Curious behind the bar. Ask him for two pints and some first principles.'

'I'm not going to talk like a prat for you. You do well enough on your own.'

The Polecat beside him had obviously heard and turned to look at Robert, who asked him about the players. They were a duo of upright bass and singer. The bassist was a golden retriever from Richmond and the vocalist a shabby cormorant from 'the back of beyond', who went under the stage name of 'The Oily Songbird'. The Polecat told Robert they were a scream.

Robert could see that Rosy was in difficulties. The bar was packed, and two large Anteaters were blocking her way but he didn't want to risk losing their seats. He left her to it.

. . .

The band began with an offbeat version of 'In A Monastery Garden', which seemed to be a favourite with the regulars. They followed with a sequence of material by Andrew Lloyd Weasel. The Songbird was particularly effective on 'Moonlight', with his carrying baritone - firm but mushy.

Robert finished his drink and realised that Rosy was still absent from his side. Also, he was about to wet his pants. He found himself next to Ian in the bogs. He'd noticed that everyone seemed to know him and that he was obviously on a promise with the lissome Polecat at their table. His wrong beginnings didn't hamper him in life. Robert's hard thinking had given him a good idea. Just ask him: trust the inspiration of the moment and the Buddha would dispose kindly in the best of all pub toilets.

'I say, er, Ian, isn't it?'

One of the boorish Anteaters came in. 'Hey, what about that tart up at t'bar? Sweet Rosemary - put the phworka in porker!'

Robert washed his hands thoroughly and managed to control himself. He found her back at their table with the drinks, chatting to the Polecat. This left him on the outer edge of things, well pissed and brooding.

'Hey, chucky egg, you know what they were saying about you in the bog?'

This was bawled, not said and the tap room quietened. 'That's right him over there, mutant ninja twathead. Sat like Stephen Fly, charming the ladies, or what passes for up here.'

Rosealea tried to ease the tension. 'He's had a rough time, strong ales, not normally like this ...'

But Ian would have none of it. 'Slaggin' our lasses when he's a pig like her in tow.'

Rosealea had had enough; she'd tried to be reasonable, but they'd asked for it. 'Robert, deck 'im.'

He had his jacket off in a trice and swaggered towards Ian in a space suddenly created by the door. The local boy felled the contender from Woodville with one blow. The beer did the rest and Robert the Bold was out cold. The band resumed with 'Love Changes Everything' as Rosealea went to her champion.

Ian apologised to her and called on his friend, Chip, to help Robert into the fresh air. Chip was a Squirrel and the local coalman. His wagon was parked out the back and Robert as laid out on some empty sacks to look at the stars.

FOUR
INCLUSION

A cold wind blows and care staff shiver
And Robert's chum goes down to the river
To see what's happened to daycare provision
And formulate a comprehensive revision.

WILLIE MOUSE WAS HOLDING AN 'INFORMAL' in the team room. 'Now, before we start, there's a postcard from the frozen north; the pubs are great for fighting and the guesthouse is the Bates Motel.'

This raised a subdued titter. 'Robert likes to embellish,' said Ted Sloth. 'I'm sure they're having fun.'

'Yes, I'm sure,' said Willie. 'Now, listen up chums. There are some bad words coming from senior management and we're going to have to be pro-active on behalf of our colleagues in day services. Something's happening somewhere.'

'Where?' inquired Ted Sloth.

'Probably down at New Leaves Day Centre. They're reviewing its function or, I believe, getting ready to close it. Then turn it over to the private sector.'

'It would be very bad to turn over New Leaves, yes,' said Otto.

'Very bad indeed,' agreed Willie, smiling. 'A significant number of our older service users rely on it - folk who might never get a lot better but who would almost certainly get worse without it.'

'Why are they moving now?' asked Ted.

'Boss Grogan's coming up to retirement, perfect chance not to replace him. Tell the users they can run it themselves and then, when it flounders, get somebody to run it cheaply or close it because the attendance has gone right down. That's generally how it's done.'

Lottie piped up to say that surely user participation and inclusiveness were valuable things and should be facilitated with boldness. Willie told her she hadn't met 'our lot'.

'Grogan's kept that place going for years. It needs some proper management now though. Ted, what have you got on today?'

'I need to talk with Bob Tail from training; he's very keen to build pathways to—'

'Not a lot. Right, you know, Boss, as well as anyone - get down there and start facilitating some roadworks with him. This is important undercover stuff and you're my top agent, a real sleeper. If you play this right, you can bugger up an entire management motorway.'

On his way downstairs, Ted met Dr. Mintoe, the scruffy terrier who headed up Psychiatry. She was showing round Dr. Beaver on her first day. Ted saw that she was lovely and wished he could forget all that. Love gave him indigestion; why couldn't it leave him alone? The wily consultant could see he was troubled. 'Are you feeling better, laddie? I hear you've been sickly again.'

'Oh fine, fine. I've taken the pledge.'

'Very wise. Now, this is Cressida who'll be working with us for a while ... perhaps she can spend time with you at some point?'

Cressida smiled at Ted as she was whisked off to see the large cupboard she'd be working from. He was feeling much better, but it didn't take much to conjure up the well of loneliness where Ted sat with his cardigan and his crossword. What on earth would a top lass like Cressida Badger want with the likes of him?

Seedy and paunchy, he slouched off towards the Woodville Ferry dwelling on the sadness of his life. He knew his simple heart hadn't mended and why he hadn't had a girlfriend since Naomi, the leggy heron two years ago. Great things had been expected and both sets of family had been involved. He would always remember when the differences in class, literary tastes, and species restriction first melted away like so much overdone stuff in a pan. That blissful memory of river Sunday, when heaven's gates were opened wide, and he could see himself as another Sloth: potent, fanciable and fast. Then one day she told him it was never going to work and flew out of his life forever. The ferry down to New Leaves Central would go past her old place but Ted knew she didn't live there anymore.

> *A sailor's yarns divert our Ted*
> *The salty dog seems off his head*
> *But wisdom comes in many guises*
> *Ted, you're in for some surprises.*

'Tickets' barked Auld Ned, the Brindle Boxer, who

conducted the ferry. Ted paid for his return fare and sat back to let two old humans ('Saps') shuffle past. A number of them lived down river from New Leaves, in an informal reservation, where they managed quite happily in township settlements with rude huts and ruder customs. Ted recalled the pilot scheme for outreach community work with them. Willie Mouse had had something to do with it and, like a lot of similar ideas, the outcome had been mixed.

Ted smiled to himself as he brought it back. It had been based on the old social work principle of reciprocity, with a nod to empowerment. The good folk of Woodville would support their country cousins, helping out with repairs and offering advice and support. An interpreter's course had been set up and began with high hopes, but the humans were mistrustful and also showed a sad tendency to neglect one another. The return was that they could be trained to do simple work in proper society and, in rare cases, taken on as pets.

This had been a sad mistake, as they fared badly away from their habitat, and had a tendency to live beyond a useful age. They were also more trouble than they were worth, with their want of constant entertainment and inability to be quiet. He knew a couple of parrots who'd taken on a female and taught her to speak. Every time Harry came home from work, she'd want to tell him about her day, then he'd have to do the same; reciprocate. It had done his head in, so Polly ran up a shroud out of old curtains. If they stood her in the corner covered up, they could watch telly in peace, but as Harry said: you *always* knew she was there.

The pair next to him were gawping vacantly across to the riverbank, where two young wallabies were yelling abuse.

Ted was firmly against cruelty to humans in all its forms

and told the 'Wallies' to show some reciprocity. As they cruised past, he heard one of them say 'fat bastard' and decided they were talking about someone else.

'No respect,' said Ned with a shake of the head. 'You must get fed up with people talking to you like that.'

'Eh, oh, I'm sure they'll grow out of it.'

'Do you get used to it though? I couldn't do your job ... slagged off in the press ... can't do right for doing wrong. No, it sometimes seems to me that what you people need ...'

Ted knew Ned from his days as a dipso bank clerk. He'd become one of Woodville's know-all's since then, ideally placed to cry up his nonsense to a captive crew. The humans looked old and tired, their plumage had faded, something was pushing them to the sides of the boat. Why did they keep going?

Ted moved up to the front of the vessel, where a scruffy lion leaned against the rail. 'Going far?' he asked.

'Knacker's Yard.'

'Does the ferry travel that far? Shady Grove's the last stop.'

'Well, let me lie in the shade and the elements may have me.'

Ted looked more closely at the tatty beast. He had a goitre and was mangy with turpentine breath and wife-beater eyes. He told him he was going to New Leaves.

'Me too,' said the Lion and proffered a paw. 'Have a look at this day centre. Brian.'

'I'm Ted. We're off to the same place then.'

Brian looked at him and frowned. 'I'm a PhD with ADHD, on top of a deliquescent personality. How about you?'

Dear God. 'I've a BA in MHP and intermittent OCD not otherwise specified.'

'Well, we're talking the same language, eh?'

'And, er, I actually work for the council.'

'We've all got something wrong with us - I'm a big believer in fighting stigma.'

Ned ambled over and Ted saw a chance to offload Brian, but the Lion moved suddenly, before Ned could speak, and made for the other end of the boat. Ted thought it could be the hyperactivity kicking in.

'You've met barmy Brian then,' said Ned.

'Yes, do you know him?'

'Lives down our road, a right case. One of your lot came to see him one time - big girl's blouse in yellow trousers. Nowt he could do.'

'Sounds like my chum, Robert Bear.'

'Aye that's him - friend of yours, eh?'

'Yes, knows his stuff, does Robert. I'm sure he gave Brian Lion a thorough psycho-social assessment.'

'Mmm. Wouldn't have him in my house.'

Ted wished he'd go away. He'd suddenly had enough of Ned's ill-bred twaddle. He finally lumbered off and Ted could see he was the fat bastard. With a running nose.

The ferry changed tack as they reached Pikey Bend and Ned came back. 'Not far now, Teddy Boy. You'll be heading for the day centre, I should think.'

'Yes, I am, actually.'

'Rather you than me. There was one used to get on - I always said she was taking the plank back to Woodville. I remember one time when she ...'

Ted had heard enough. 'Presumably this one had a name?'

'Doris Bonkers. Not her real name like, though she had been known to answer to it.'

'A slightly built seagull by any chance?'

'Yes, that's the one. It's coming back now. Did she ever ...?'

'I happen to know her, and she's had enough to put up with without your coarse mockery. She's called Persephone by the way.'

Ned noticed that he was being challenged. 'Let's not fall out; a ship's imperiled when the sailors disagree. It's just bluff mariners' talk, so take no heed, sir.'

Arse, thought Ted. The old josser had spent his working life blissfully pushing paper round a desk at the Woodville and Forest Town Building Society before they weighed him off into a retirement job. The ferry company must have seen him as just the sort of personality to pull in the boat going public. They couldn't have known.

'I don't think a life on the ocean wave is any excuse for bad behaviour, you know.'

'Oh, she wasn't to know and, besides, as every Jack Tar can tell you, seagulls have always flown too close to the moon. Dirty beggars too.'

'Don't you think that we're all in the same boat?'

'How's that then, Ted?'

I ought to value his individuality thought Ted. After all, he'd be valuing difference, celebrating whatever it was he believed in. It would be the right thing to do and, as he knew, if you did the right thing, the right thing sometimes happened.

They were close to their destination. New Leaves Central showed itself as a pagoda-style building of locally sourced redwood. It was picked out demurely in pale sunlight and as he enjoyed the sight, Ted remembered a nice little branch of 'Cake Hole' had been open last time he'd been. He hadn't had time for toast that morning and thought a chat with Ned would also go towards his research. He wasn't that keen on actually visiting the day centre and wouldn't be that bothered if it got the chop - a mare's nest of dangerous characters and lefty string-alongs presided over by dodgy Boss Grogan. It was Ted's view that you could take diversity too far if you weren't careful.

'What time do we set sail back to Woodville, Ned?'

'Not till twelve, though I've a ship's inspection before then.'

'But you've time for a cuppa first?'

'I should think so.'

The Woodville Ferry's real commander, a lithe Chimpanzee, danced about by the wheelhouse and shut down 'The Leviathans' engine. The passengers all stood before they needed to and formed a line.

Ted couldn't see Brian and asked a Hare at the back if he'd seen him. 'Sat in the stern, didn't look too clever.'

Ted found him embracing a pile of rope, trying to ward off the jitters. Someone else had left a paper bag nearby full of cigarette stubs and discarded tissues. Ted tipped as much as he could over the side and gave the bag to Brian, telling him to take deep breaths. Then they sat together till it was over. Ted saw a fag end lodged in Brian's whiskers but didn't want to cause him anymore trouble.

'Your mate get off alright?' asked Ned.

'Yeah. Taken a lot out of him really - getting here today.'

'Done him a good turn then; mind, that's only what you're paid for.'

'Doing good?'

'Aye, good job you were there an' all, but it doesn't always work, does it, and most folk could have done what you did, couldn't they?'

Ted knew he must get at least one third of his strawberry cheesecake down before the lumbering libertarian hit his stride.

Ned slurped his cappuccino as he looked out the window. Some rough merboys had surfaced outside and were throwing stones at the Chimp. 'You watch. Jacko'll sort 'em out,' said Ned.

As Ted saw, the skipper dealt quite roughly with the cheeky boys, hurling one into the wheelhouse and striking another about the head as he escaped over the side.

'I blame the parents of course.' Ned was off. 'When I was a pup, me Dad would—'

'You said that anyone could have helped Brian - but nobody did.'

'Why, if you hadn't, someone else would have.'

'You sure?'

'Yes, why not?'

'They might have, but then again ... I know one thing. We'll never be out of work in my trade.'

The merboys reappeared on the wooden decking outside. Ted assumed that the lad limping with blood leaking from his head must have been the one Jacko threw about the ferry. He looked right enough.

'So,' said Ned eventually. 'Why do you bother?'

Ted had been running out of answers to that one, particularly for his lazy brother Lucien, a fitful autodidactic who lived at home and told Ted that he was 'a useful idiot of the revisionist state'. At least Ned got out of the house. He was at it again. 'I mean a lot of people might think you're a bunch of useless idiots for the nanny state. Mind you, there's plenty of idiots about these days.'

'Yes,' said Ted. 'Anyway, I sometimes wonder myself. I think we all do; I know Robert does. You can never seem to do enough of whatever it is people say they want, and people only ever come to us when they're fed up, to begin with. You must get happy travelers on the ferry - folk that *want* to be there.'

'Hardly the same. My job's just to get them from one end o' t'river to t'other - the happy ones have generally come on board from The Rats Whiskers. It's just helping them on their way.'

'That's all I want to do though. Why doesn't it always work out like that?'

Ned fished out his bosun's pipe and plugged in some 'Smugglers Moon'. After a fair bit of tamping and thumbing, he got the thing going. 'Well, the Social Services are the conscience of society.'

But Ted wasn't listening. He was somewhere else, recovering lost time on his father's knee. The old man was puffing out clouds of pungent smoke while he read little Ted stories about dancing scarecrows and the Powdered Toastman who was always running from the Scrambled Egg Baby.

'Is my smoke bothering you?'

'No, no, it's fine. It's just you don't often smell that these days. I like it, really.'

'Yes, anyway, generally speaking, you're doing a job folk would rather not know about, but if you get it wrong, they do then they're angry with you. And it's always your fault.'

'Sometimes, it is.'

'You know that lass we were talking about earlier – Percyphone? She said summat once that made sense for a change. I've remembered it.'

Ted waited while Ned puffed more clouds of memory and

wondered why a pipe on the go conferred wisdom on the puffer. It just did and Ned's seductive smoke was working its magic. '"We need never be perfectly miserable so long as we can do a good-natured action".'

'She said that?'

'She said that. She was quoting Sir Philip Siskin, a wise old bird from days of yore. I bet he'd never known a girl like her.'

'I dare say. You know, the poets have much to tell us if only we can remember. Know any more pillars of wisdom?'

They were both enjoying themselves.' Right, here's another. "If we were to do good it were best done in small measures ..." - so said William Drake.'

'Like running an efficient ferry.'

'If you like. I clapped eyes on some fondant fancies when we came in. Good in small measures they are.'

Fresh drinks and cakes came and went, then it was time for Ned to take some people up stream. Ted went for a pee and settled himself on a bench by the river to work out how to take his new ideas to the day centre. The passive inhalation of pipe smoke, the lardy cakes and warm sun caused Ted to feel woozy, so he closed his eyes.

Ted's dream began along lines that were hardly subconscious or in need of interpretation. He was moving through Woodville with the nippiness of a mouse and the sexual capacity of a guinea pig on short measures. Girls of various kinds fell at his feet. Then more troubling visions came along. He was lost in a hall of mirrors and each reflection seemed wrong, then Rosealea appeared smoking a pipe. She pouted and puffed the smoke into letters he couldn't read. He didn't have his trousers on, and he was straining to pee in a squalid toilet full of large mutant insects slithering and clicking around him. One of them spoke in a Parrot's voice, 'do it small daddy'.

He woke up and forgot what he'd heard but the dream's ambience of mouldy cake and toilet pong lingered. He revisited the clean white facilities by the café, felt better, and went for a restorative cup of coffee. He knew there was nothing doing down the day centre. An elegant Stork caught his eye, lifting its lovely legs in and out of the riverside mud, reminding him of Naomi. Thoughts on the vagaries of the animal heart returned him to the image of Rosealea and he caught a faint echo of a faint echo of the dream. Something to do with intensely thwarted desire and her mocking laughter. Robert was his rival as well as his chum, and he really was a jammy sod having all that loveliness to himself.

Ted had been after her for months, building his bower with small but pointed chat in the kitchen, a supportive debrief after she'd thrown things round the office in reaction to a tricky piece of work, well-judged words on her regular rows with all and sundry. Then she went on a training weekend with Robert to Peewit's training facility, which also turned out to be a well-known cop-off facility, and that was it. The smooth-talking devil had stolen her from under his nose - talk about experiential learning. He'd heard that love changed everything, so when was he going to get some?

'You still here then?' It was Ned, back on dry land again.

'Yes, I'll come back up stream with you.'

'Climb aboard sir; you'll find your sea legs where you left them.'

Ted sat down on a bench near the rear and watched the other passengers boarding. He saw the Lion telling something to an Anteater in a top hat. Brian looked a bit happier, and the

Anteater was laughing. They both made their way in Ted's direction and Brian sat beside him.

'Alright, mate?' he asked.

'Not so bad, and yourself?'

'I've been included.'

'Oh, aye.'

'At the day centre. Been empowered an' all.'

'Many there then?'

'Packed out. There was a big meeting about fighting the cuts, folk were really lit up - especially when the man from the mental health team didn't show up as promised. His loss. There was a turn at lunch time and a nightingale got up to sing about how you never know what you've got till it's gone, and it all had to do with big taxes. Brilliant. They'll have to think again now, eh?'

Ned had appeared at this point as he moved among his ship, giving out random comments and free association banter. Ted made a point of telling him how much he'd learned at the day centre. Ned gave him a funny look, then got caught up with a small pug dog who wanted to know if they could shoot an albatross on the way home. Ned hadn't seen one for years and, anyway, political correctness had spoiled all that.

Ted looked across as they passed 'Three Sheets' care home. An old Fox in a bonnet was tottering towards the water with a vacant smile and was caught at the last moment by a harassed looking Chicken.

Brian saw it too. 'Wouldn't it be kinder just to let 'em go?'

'Depends what sort of society you want to live in,' said Ted.

'So they say,' agreed Brian.

Ted knew he'd have to do some homework for Willie

Mouse. 'What about the day centre? You said you'd felt included?'

'Eh, oh, I was just having a laugh. Nobody really says that apart from the boobies at County Hall.'

'They're alright though, aren't they? Try to do the right thing. Can't be easy for them?'

'Easier than it is for most folk.'

'But they can help, can't they?'

Brian sat up a bit straighter. 'Oh, yeah, but they're never going to get three cheers because the damage has always been done - certainly has in my case. They're never going to set us right again, but if they let us keep the day centre and leave us alone to get on with it, we'll muddle through. Or move into recovery, if you prefer.'

Pretending not to be a social worker made Ted see Brian in a different light. They could have been each other, or anybody. Was this normalisation and was it challenging him to find some new ways of working? He didn't know and felt like chucking his satchel into the River Nut. 'This place made you feel better then?'

'It did today. If they keep it open, I'll go again?'

'What was so good about it?'

Ted could see that he was annoying him, but he was used to that. It was a form of engagement after all.

'Come along and see for yourself. Join the Barmy Army - give the paper shufflers at County Hall something to think about.'

'What's the Barmy Army?'

'Our action group watch out for us down your way. Now, thanks for being Johnny On the Spot earlier on, but I'm off Mr. Slope.'

. . .

They drifted slowly up the lazy river and Ted began to shape his thoughts into some kind of narrative - a believable story for his manager, stressing the diverse feedback taken and the undercover research into a prototype anarchist group. On the way to the gents below deck, Ted reflected on the skills required to get people to accept an emotional truth when the facts might be open to interpretation.

He found Ned telling a party of Rabbits about the stirring events of '62, when the town had been 'taken at the flood' and a heroic pack of local Dogs had ensured that vital supplies had 'got through'.

When he went back up on deck, Ted saw the lights of Woodville landing showing through some willow trees. He went to find Brian and saw him chatting quite calmly to a turkey. As he approached, he caught the tail end of something the bubbly jock was saying. '... right load of rubbish from what I can see.'

'Hi,' greeted Brian. 'We were just talking about the limits of welfareism. Tommy reckons that all you can do is generate the conditions for hope, then leave folk to get on with it.'

'I'm sure he's right,' said Ted.

By the time Ted got back to the office most people had left, though he did find Lottie patting a keyboard, so he stopped to chat. She was putting up a direct-payments assessment for a troubled cat with no money and wanted to get it on file directly. He also found out that manager Mouse was out and not expected back.

He went off to his own desk and produced a clean sheet of lined paper. Seen from the doorway and viewed beneath the mysterious warmth of the angle poise lamp, Ted's task would have looked solemn and binding. The kind of thing a Sloth might be required to do but once in a lifetime and, when it came, the Sloth had to be ready. Under the heading of 'A Voyage into New Waters' Ted wrote of many things - reflections on self-directed day services, lookout for hope, costed proposals, bespoke provision, new light on the delta. And locally sourced cakes.

FIVE
SOMETHING IN THE AIR

The day's set fair, the clouds disperse
And Robert Bear is none the worse
For bracing walks and serious talks
But here is where the old road forks.

'LOOK, it's been great, and I'll remember to pass that message on to your brother.' Robert tapped his button nose and Ratty grinned.

'Aye, well, it's been nice having you and I'm sorry about them moles - right pair of cowboys.'

Rosealea appeared in her going-home outfit: a purple tweed two-piece suit as might have been worn by a lady almoner of 1948. It had been bought on an estrogen fueled whim at Newcastle market and was topped off by a straw hat with stuck-on wax fruit. 'What's he givin' it now?' she asked.

'The decorators. Like quite a bit round here, knocked up on a whim.'

'A bit like me then.'

'I wasn't thinking ...'

'No.'

He looked at the clock on the wall. A nice bit of tat lending halfhearted gentility to the doss house from Hades. Its gaudy fingers showed half-past nine, another ninety minutes before Rosey's poise should return. She'd been awful during the week and he'd been unable to do anything right till mid-morning. He was keen to get them up in the air as soon as possible. 'Now, I've loaded everything and it's a fine fresh morning. Do you fancy breaking the journey again?'

'Nah, let's get straight back, I feel a bit bleurrgh ...' She coughed up a goodbye deposit on the doorstep.

'Don't mind that, pet,' called Ratty from a bedroom window. 'I'll see to it - youse get off.'

'Christ. Rob, just get that pissing plane going.'

As they went up and away from the recreation field, a group of baby Elephants trumpeted their farewell - a ragged but affecting version of 'In the Mood'. The visitors were soon a dot in the sky.

'Okay, pet,' bawled the pilot.

'Just get us home.'

Robert thought about the holiday. That spot of bother on the first night didn't seem so bad anymore; he'd buff it up into a serviceable anecdote. The obvious highlight had been the visit to Castle Bladderack, built as a front-line defense against invading beavers, then a seat of great learning under King Bob. He'd planned the whole thing carefully and brushed up on the literature.

Bob the Second was the best known of the House of Hog, which ruled this part of the world in days of yore. A time of sustained peace and commercial success, and Bob had been dubbed 'Cognito Grandioso' or 'Mighty Thinker'. He had

encouraged the growth of early learning centers and Bladderack had seen the earliest ones which had, over time, become
a great treasure trove of relics. These included the 'Shroud of
Shields' and archetypes from the 'legends of sacking'; he had
caught Rosealea's interest with strands from the mangled
weave of local folklore.

The weave showed itself to be threadbare and faded. The
shroud had been an unlikely myth, featuring visions by the sea
and a Cow with five legs. There was a dull naïve painting of a
vague shape in the sky and several effigies that could have been
anything. The legend endured in bottles of fortified wine,
which were on sale in the shop. It had been a laugh and they'd
gone off for a nice cake and cup of 'Bobs' in the café where they
decided to see the 'sacking' material.

The relevant part of the castle had been a bit like one of the
smaller and smarter parts of the Old Professor's place. The first
surprise was that sacking meant sex, which itself turned out to
be a derivative of the earlier word. There were some stunning
illustrations in the style of the Bearude tapestries and some
unfettered accounts of sex life in the fourteenth century.

What had really gripped Robert and Rosealea were a series
of woven images titled 'Randomiun Natalis' or 'Birthday
Surprises'. They showed miscegenation and crossbreeding on a
scale to make modern pairings seem tame. According to the
squares, not only did the lion lay down with the lamb but owls
did it with fish from the sea, goats fell for horses. Even human
forms could be seen getting in on the act, but this was felt to be
disgraceful and the devil's work.

Old Nick himself could even be found skulking about in
the background of one of the images. Robert had pointed out
his resemblance to Barry Fox from work and she'd chortled

then stopped abruptly at the next frame. It featured a bear and a hog with their baby. This had been a moving experience for them. At first sight, the baby looked a bit like a waxy cherub left too long by the fire. The parents seemed happy enough and a closer look at the child hinted at porcine guile and playfulness. Its little face showed piggy eyes with a button nose, floppy ears and a neat little mouth. The body was wrapped in golden swaddling, but they'd seen enough. The baby had been called Edmund and Rosealea was entranced.

Robert looked at the fuel gauge and decided there'd be enough to get them home. Down below he could see the remains of 'Droppings', the giant folly put up in the nineteenth century by a donkey dynasty from Dudley. They'd been ironmasters but a terrible falling out had ruined the business and the place had been left to rot. He'd always wanted to go there and look for human traces of the tragic engineers from the wild West Midlands. He could see his windy passenger lolling in the back.

'My place or yours?' he called.

'Don't care; which is nearest?'

They thundered along, then the little red man came on, waving a warning finger on the dashboard. Robert muttered 'fuck' at him, then the outskirts of Greater Woodville came into view. He took them down towards the field behind Rosealea's house. It was a rough landing and shook the returning holidaymakers.

'Are you trying to induce a miscarriage, you useless Herbert?'

'Sorry, pet - bit of turbulence on the way down.'

'Don't call me that,' she said, then stalked off towards the back garden.

He stood open-mouthed, like a husband outside a shop. *What do you want me to do?* Then an arsey farmer called out from the other side of a five-bar gate, 'What's the game, Biggles?'

'Sorry - emergency landing with a sick passenger.'

'Aye, well, just get it shifted.'

'I'm nearly out of fuel.'

'With a sick passenger - you don't seem on the ball, mate. Anyway I need this field for pasture, so look sharp.'

Robert looked about the field - mostly nettles and discarded fencing with some rusty corrugated panels. He was cross enough to give back at the guy but when he turned round, the farmer, another long-legged Terrier, had gone. He was on his own.

There was more to unload than there had been to pack when they'd left. Rosealea's trips round the charity shops and markets of Tyneside had brought in a bumper haul and Robert's own bookshop idylls had turned up a slim volume or two. One of these was a full-length edition of *In My Good Books* - Edward Gibbon's nine-volume history of all the world's greatest thinkers. He'd already looked at the first book and read about the stoic poodles of Brittany. There was so much to learn.

He looked up as he lumbered the first load down the long garden; she was jabbering on the phone. He called through to let her know that as soon as he'd got all the luggage up, he would be shifting the plane.

'Whatever,' she called. 'I'll be having a lie down.'

He wondered how a stoic Bear would react. He didn't like to think of Rosy as a lazy pig and concentrated on how well he'd piloted them and cleared the fence, first go, on the way out of the farmer's field. He came down neatly at the garage, but

Mr. Rat wasn't about, and the Saturday lad couldn't say when he would be back.

'Have I to fill her up chief?' asked the young Stoat.

Robert gave him the nod and asked the youth if anything much had happened while he'd been away.

'Well, you know Woodville ... landlord put on a new barrel at 'The Squinting Cat' and there was some kerfuffle on at Town Hall.'

Robert showed some interest. 'Kerfuffle?'

'Some kind of demonstration got out of hand. PC Penguin had to blow his whistle then there was rough stuff from some of the protesters - a window went through. My dad works there, and he says that the protest had been hijacked by BAMBI.'

'Who are they? This doesn't have anything to do with firearms, does it?'

'No, but my dad reckons it might have. BAMBI is the name of a local lefty group - layabouts and wrong 'uns. My dad says—'

'Yes, but what does it stand for?'

'Dunno but my—'

'Where does your father work at County Hall?'

'Parks and Gardens - near you, is that?'

'No, I'm upstairs in Mental Health.'

The lad's demeanor changed and he went into the small office before Robert could pay him. He left the money under a stone by the door. As he made the short flight to his own house, Robert wondered what else the lad's father came out with.

Back at home Robert sifted through his mail. A week away, but the only sign of change in his little house was the full bowl from a dripping tap. His holiday reading had left its mark and he tried to see this small image as the slow drip of domestic life. Or had it been diurnal? He found his little book and jotted it down in both versions. These observations were building up nicely, rather like a dripping tap he thought as he emptied the bowl. Perhaps he should call the eventual collection 'Notes from A Drip'.

He'd talked to Rosealea while they were away about his special thoughts. She'd scoffed but he'd explained that if he had the silks of heaven, he could lay them before her but, as he only had his dreams, she'd better tread softly on them. That had shut her up. So what if he was sometimes a 'precious tosser'; he was what he was and could be no other. He had a wash and brush up, then set off to walk across town to Rosey's place at Weeping Cross. He bumped into Tiger Lily down the precinct.

'Hi Lobert, how you doin?' said the friendly Chinese lass.

'Pretty good. Just been away for a week at Redcar.'

'You so lucky, man. The song of the sea bring comfort to those what need it, eh?'

'So they say.'

'I think the old 'fessor need to see the sea. Maybe you hear from us next week. *Ciao* Lobee.'

Robert arrived at Rosealea's house refreshed and keen to tell her his news. After she'd listened politely, he summed up along the lines of 'ructions at work' and the Prof relapsing.

She was dubious. 'Well, if you can believe anything Tokyo Rose comes out with, let alone the word of some gormless youth who hides from Robert Bear.'

'It was his dad's word, as he kept saying.'

'I think I know who his father is,' said Rosealea. 'Bit of a wiseacre, got caught up in that cherub-shooting club.'

'With your Uncle Pete.'

'He wasn't there, so I've an open mind on all that.'

. . .

They were sitting in her open plan lounge, eating from trays as the final scores came through. Woodville had won away at Fallow Field - 'a sensational last-minute goal from Ben Sloth, the 'Nutters' nippy winger.'

'Would he be related to Ted at work?' asked Rosealea.

'Might be. Could you imagine Ted as a nippy footballer?'

She laughed. 'I thought he might kick the bucket when he went off sick you know. He looked awful. You went to see him, didn't you?'

Robert swallowed his mouthful of spud pie. 'He was completely rundown, poor sod. They reckoned he'd got a dose of that ME thing, probably depressed too. Either way, he was completely knackered, even for him. He went up a tree in the park and didn't come down for a week.'

'Not even to go to the bog?'

'No, but apparently they only need to go every three weeks or so and if you're off your food, well, you could last longer.'

'Mmm, but what was the story?'

'A broken heart. Then there was that bad do with Gaffer Jarge and the community treatment order expiring - caught Ted napping - and I think he's always been prone to melancholy.'

'A broken heart, him?'

'Oh yes, he'd been going out with this heron called Natasha, bit of a flighty piece. Good looker mind and he took it bad when she marked his card.'

'What's on telly tonight?'

Robert looked in his weekly guide. The main choices were Pro-Celebrity cherub tossing, Inspector Mouse or 'It's A Lock Out', a worthy but dull history of industrial relations in days of yore. Mouse got the nod, but first Robert washed up and sided away, then they had sex on the rug, Rosealea's interest having picked up.

They were ready by eight and settled down to watch the latest episode featuring the wily but anti-social Inspector Mouse and his Geordie sidekick, Louse. It was called 'Are You Having A Laugh?' and turned out to be a classy production with proper music and clever camerawork. The story featured a comedian who literally died on stage and some German poetry, which Robert couldn't place in the plot. Mouse got it of course when he was doing a crossword in a pub and making Louse look soft. The finale saw the two detectives tied together in a dark and grubby cellar with ominous noises coming from above. Louse asked Mouse if this was their Armageddon and Mouse told him not to worry as it wasn't the end of the world. The heavy Gerbil, who was keeping them there, laughed so much he fell over and fractured his skull on a handy boiler.

'That was a touch of genius, sir,' said Louse.

'Are the pubs open yet?' inquired Mouse.

Rosealea was impressed. 'Oh, he's very good, is Mouse. You'll not get topside of him in a murder investigation. Canny as owt.'

Robert enjoyed the films too but considered Mouse a posturing pillock with his Wagner and his red Roller. 'Don't you think Louse would get there faster without his boss quoting Virgil at every opportunity?'

'Now you really are 'avin a laugh, lover.'

He smiled and joined in with a good natured roustabout before bed.

He was disturbed in the early hours by Rosy retching in the bathroom. He got up to show willing, but she told him she was 'off it again' and sent him back to bed. Later on, she held him close and asked him what they'd started. Robert was relieved, his breezy don't-fret-pet had been good enough on holiday but now they were back at home and things were different. He fussed and fondled her, then got up to make breakfast, as would any proper partner.

He hadn't been able to tell how much good he'd done, and the rest of their Sunday had been a bit hit and miss. There'd been a bracing walk, followed by a pub lunch, a nice nap, then a gentle spot of gardening, but she'd not been herself. He'd caught her a couple of times looking at him with an expression of strain, and her tittering at his jokes had been flat.

Things became clearer when 'Antiques Express' came on after tea. Fiona Fox had been presenting the popular show from 'the beautiful county town of Cockfast'. Robert had said how nice it would be to be there among the mullioned windows and period-style McDonalds.

'And would you be there for me with the fair Fiona simpering in your cloth ear?'

'Erm no, I mean yes, but where does she fit into the picture?'

'Well, isn't it all like something off the tele to you?'

Robert misjudged the moment. 'You mean mistaking the wish for the deed, not always connecting with external—'

'Don't you talk to me like that, I've told you before.'

He'd got it then. 'Sorry, Rosy.'

'This is our baby. I need to know what you feel about it all. Not have to guess what your daft cracks might mean.'

'I think it's great, honestly, and maybe it was meant to be.'

'For all we know, it could be a right little horror with WDD and MFI, or whatever else they've come up with by then. I saw Satan working some mischief in those tapestries.'

'Are WDD and MFI the devil's works then?'

'Wilful Disobedience Disorder and Mysteriously Functioning Infant. They describe a cluster of symptoms but very little is known about them. Crossbreeding is strongly associated and some of them with MFI are very high functioning, but quite rare. What do you think the chances are of you and I hitting the jackpot?'

'Rosy, I love you very much and I want you to have my babies, however they turn out.'

She came towards him to rest her head on his shoulder. He put a paw to her nice warm ear, and to his amazement, they had it off again. Downstairs too. He was blissfully fatigued afterwards and lay panting on her lovely pink belly.

'I want to move in here with you,' he managed eventually.

'Well,' she said. 'We've managed a week away at Redcar.'

'I ought to nip home and get some stuff for tomorrow.'

'Nip in the morning, then you can give me a lift in.'

'Alright.'

SIX
I'VE GOT A GOOD IDEA

The best intentions of hens and bears
Are marred by careless thinking
Many an effort towards the right thing
Is scotched by lunch-time drinking.

'IF YOU WANT TO, I'll change the situation, right people right time ... boom-boom, my son.'

'You are in a jolly mood this morning, Herr Sloth.'

'Morning. Otto that I am, and please call me Ted. I'm on a mission with this day centre business. I really feel I could be so good for them.'

'Were you involved in last week's enlivenments?'

'No, not directly but there's a tide in the affairs of day care.'

Otto looked at Ted. 'It was the case that damage occurred and horses frightened, I think.'

'Just a few hot heads. You always get them; they'll not be back.'

'Were the hotheads not organised and intent on trouble?'

'No, of course not, it was just indicative of the strength of people's feelings, and that should have been anticipated.'

'Perhaps Herr Mouse knows more.'

Their manager came into the team room with Robert, who took Otto aside to tell him all about Redcar. Willie Mouse asked Ted to go to his office.

On the way out, he heard Robert saying, 'She had to pull me off 'im.'

He joined the boss, who closed the door behind him.

'Right agent, Ted, tell me again what happened when you visited New Leaves last week.'

Ted could barely remember what he'd told Willie and decide to come clean. 'I never actually got to the centre, you know. It was all a bit ...'

'Of a doss. If you had got there, you might have encountered several members of BAMBI planning rough stuff and mayhem.'

'What is BAMBI, Boss?'

'Bad news, Ted. It was them behind all that rumpus last week, pushing and shoving on the Town Hall steps. Anarchists, in Woodville, that's all we need.'

'Is Boss Grogan in on it? That wouldn't be like him.'

'I doubt it, they've just taken advantage. BAMBI stands for Beasts Against Malign Bureaucracy Init. They are run by 'Red Robin' and are on the move. We know they have infiltrated some important parts of Woodville's establishment. For all I know, they could have turned you. Would make sense - a useful dupe to be sacrificed later, a harmless dreamer with little understanding of the real world. Wouldn't you say, eh?'

Ted was glad his carpeting had started; it would soon be over. 'But what are they up to down at New Leaves?'

'That's what I want you to find out. You and Rockin''

Robert - I hear he's been hardened by his Teesside holiday. He can put it to good use on those lawless roads.'

Once they'd landed at County Hall, Rosealea had made straight for the ladies, locking herself in a cubicle.

It wasn't long before 'Nursie' Wilson, one of the CP Hens, came into the adjacent cubicle. She heard snuffles and called softly, 'Are you alright, dear?'

Rosealea paused, then asked who was there.

'It's me, Bantam Wilson. I've come to see Salome. Can I help?'

'Dunno.'

'Do you want to tell me?'

Rosealea blew her snout, hitched herself up and pulled back the catch with a sharp clack.

Nurse Bantam was waiting for her. 'I'll find a quiet room, eh?'

Rosealea nodded vacantly and followed Nursie into one of the small interview rooms on the ground floor, where she told her the news. She'd been up in the night with sharp pains and found she was passing blood. It had just happened again but without the pains. She knew she was going to miscarry. She was advised not to despair as it could be that her baby had simply changed position. How pregnant was she and who was the father?

The answers to these questions made Nursie look thoughtful and make a phone call, though there was still nothing to worry about.

A not unpleasant state of mind began to soothe Rosealea. Nothing seemed to matter; was this what he'd been on about?

She sat and watched Robert and Ted through the window. They were having a serious talk in the car park. She wondered if he might be telling a trusted chum all about it. They went back in. Ted looked thoughtful.

'Right,' said Nursie when she returned. 'I've called in a few favours and they can scan you at Woodville General. Mr. Spaniel will see you at ten. He's the top dog in obstetrics.'

'But what's wrong?'

'Probably nothing and that's what we can verify, but you're probably carrying quite an unusual baby.'

'Oh, yes?'

'With a Bear and a Pig, the foetus can grow quickly. You're probably further on than you think. Have you been feeling more tired than usual and keener on cakes?'

'You ... what? Well, now you mention it ...'

'Come on, Rose. I'll run you down there.'

'Does he want us to infiltrate this group then, be like moles? I'm part mole myself, you know.'

Robert was scornful. 'I don't see it, do you? The sloth who came in from the cold.'

'Yes, I suppose you're right, Robert.'

'Don't let tatty whiskers get to you; come on, let's go in.'

'It's not just him. I'm sexually frustrated. I can't get a girl-friend ... you're so lucky to have Rosy cheeks.'

'Look, let's get this day centre business sorted, then we'll go for a drink, eh?'

'Yes.'

By the time Nursie brought them down at the hospital on her fiery Kimono Japanese job (put together in Sunderland),

Rosealea's cheeks were pasty, and she felt awful. She'd had her fill of flying. 'I don't think there's much point, Bant; you're wasting your morning on me.'

'We're here now; it's just over there.'

'In that portakabin?'

'No, that's the hospital social workers. See that smart clinic? Over there?'

By the time she was lying down with someone plastering blue goo on her belly, Rosealea was feeling properly looked after. She began to relax, then a trolley appeared beside her with a monitor. The scan began as the obstetric nurse moved the camera across her womb and asked Mrs. Pig if she could feel her baby's heart beating.

'I don't know, call me Rosy.'

'It's that regular bleep and ... yes, look at the screen. Can you see?'

Rosy was unprepared for the precious little face that looked back at her and the perfect tiny hand moving slowly in her direction. She lifted a trotter in reply, then burst into tears. She also caught a fleeting impression of a vague memory of the Bladderack tapestries. It was enough.

Mr. Spaniel came in and the nurses became more businesslike as he looked with authority at the scan and asked Rosy some stuff about times, dates and fathers. He sat down to scratch his left ear and deliver his verdict. 'Given the timescales and unusual pairing, plus what is known so far about left-field conceptions, you are comfortably on course for a healthy female hybridus mirabilis some time ... next week.'

'You're having a laugh - next week, how come? I want another opinion; this can't be right. I only found out meself last week.'

'You'll get the same news. I know it's a shock, but it all seems to have something to do with the genetic synergy.

Nature's, or love's, way of breaking the rules, throwing in a wild card. I wonder if you'll let me write it up.'

'Why not? Better be quick though. Do they grow up fast once they're out?'

'To be honest, we're not sure which is why you and your baby are so interesting. Here, have a picture.'

'Thank you, I'll need that to show the father. You're sure it's a little lass?'

'Positive.'

On the way back to work, Rosealea was full of praise for Nursie and told her they might call the baby Banty. She was advised to talk to Robert.

'Oh, there'll be some talking there. Next week, next pissing week - we've nowt to eat. His lot can pitch in 'cos mine'll be neither use nor ornament. Seven days.'

'He did say sometime next week ... it's not forced to be Monday.'

'Monday's child is fair of face, look at this picture. I can't wait to show Robby.'

The soon-to-be-proud father was alighting from the Woodville ferry at that moment with his colleague Agent Sloth. Ned, the skipper, had said welcome aboard on the way downstream and, as the only other passengers had been a dowdy bunch of saps, Robert had shown an interest. The Saps had settled in the prow and bickered throughout the journey, as they tended to do whenever they went outside the reservation.

Robert knew that there was quite a settlement near New Leaves and could remember being brought as a child to hear the singing festivals they would put on. They had lapsed and he wondered if some kind of outreach project might be set up via the day centre to rekindle some of the older connections between beast and man. The few who had integrated, like Gaffer Jarge or the wheezy old boy who sold tickets at the train station, tended to be shunned by their own kind. The Old Professor of course, was an exception as nobody that clever could be fully human, and he knew how to talk to the animals.

Robert found Ted gazing wistfully at the riverbank. 'The old dog's value for money isn't he? Certainly knows a thing or two about masts and keel-hauling.'

Ted laughed. 'Most of its seaman's twaddle. I've heard him belting out 'The Sailors Hornpipe' and he got it wrong, B is for Boson, not barnacle, and S marks the spot where old Sparky was drowned. There were several others.'

Robert remembered how stressed his chum could get when there was a big job on. 'Well, we're here now, let's see what we might be able to do.'

'I don't know what Willie thinks that might be.'

The path to the day centre took them along the edge of a wood screening off the saps. Their sad sounds filtered through the forest: 'fucktwat fuck fuck twat'. They were the town's dark secret, and their belligerent cries had a feral quality, a hint of the bad things running beneath Woodville's smooth topsoil.

Ted moved ahead and led them out into a sunnier patch with a stream and children at play. They crossed over and soon found a developed area with shops and a library. The day centre was next door, a purpose-built job put up in better days, with an abstract sculpture above the door signifying acceptance and recovery. Robert has always thought it looked like a goal-keeper missing the ball.

Inside, they encountered a phoenix and a turtle smoking

roll-ups and passed on down a corridor to a large hall with a stage. A harassed pigeon was hopping out on one leg and told them it had been 'hell on wheels' since last week's carry on.

'We've just come down from County Hall to see if we can help. Is Boss about?'

The lame bird looked at them suspiciously and Ted asked him if he was a member of the tendency.

'Eh? Are you after a good pecking or what?'

Boss Grogan appeared, a greying red setter of advanced years. 'What's cracking off? Morning lads, hope you're not upsetting anyone.'

'No,' replied Ted. 'I was meaning the militant tendency, you know trouble down the town hall, sod the council.'

He'd lowered his voice to emphasize his point. Boss ignored him and looked around the room as Woodville folk began to drift in. 'Well, there's militant Martin, the red squirrel; he knows all about Staling and the great terror, but I can't see that catching on, here can you?'

Robert and Ted smiled, then Boss directed them to his office while he helped the group outside set up. 'The programme is for a discussion group, 'What the Papers Say'. It generally concludes that you can't believe half of what you read in the press, but plenty of warmth and communion is engendered on route.'

Ted got them tea from the machine while his chum made himself comfortable. Robert had never envied the life of a day centre manager: no urgent visits when you were fed up with the office, or vice versa, social workers not returning your calls when something was wrong, supervising the staff and what happened if people wouldn't go home at four o' clock? He'd often felt a bit of a nit in Boss' presence and sat up straight when he came in with Ted.

'Just need to make a quick one,' he said and picked up the phone.

From what could be heard, the business involved onions and reciprocity.

'That was the Magic Bean food co-operative. They're interested in a deal whereby we supply them with produce from the allotment group and they cut us in on some special offers. Now, what's all this foolish prattle about reds under our strawberry beds?'

Ted went first. 'It seems that BAMBI has a foothold in the centre and was heavily involved in the demo in the town, steering the action towards a bad outcome.'

Boss couldn't hide his scorn. 'Well, old BAMBI would have a paw-hold, wouldn't she? And as for getting it behind the steering wheel of anarchy – nah, not the Bambi I knew.'

Robert spoke. 'That demo was a roughhouse you know.'

'Listen lads, I was there, and it was handbags in the afternoon. As for BAMBI, I think you're probably referring to BIMBO.'

'Oh, crikey,' groaned Ted. 'Who are they when they're at home?'

Boss explained. 'A hardline feminist outfit: Bints Insist Men Bog Off. I'm sure they have infiltrated the centre, but I'm not that bothered. I reckon I know who they are and as long as they behave, they're probably a positive influence.'

Ted was flustered. 'But what about their works, these busters? Sounds like bad news to me. I knew a funny mist once—'

'Teddy boy,' said Boss with a sigh. 'Remember the social workers glossary of bollocks?'

'Yes,' laughed Robert. 'The new edition has a chapter on

how to speak nicely to people. It's called 'Highways and Byways of Vernacular Discourse'.

'Yes,' said Boss. 'Fresh and steaming ... what I was thinking about was respecting diversity, working with difference. You know, getting on with folk even if they seem soft in the head.'

'Even when they daub things?'

'What do you mean, Ted?' asked Robert.

'Never trust a man with bollocks. I've seen it in the town.'

'Oh I've seen that - down by the footie ground. Was that them then, Boss?'

'Aye, like as not but they're not bothered with argy-bargy or anything like that. Keener on rumination. They're right enough really, probably seen some things in their time, poor souls.'

'Right,' said Ted. 'Why should the centre survive?'

'Come and find out,' invited Boss.

Their first stop was the discussion group where a cowed-looking penguin was flapping its little arms over something in the Mail. Ted's friend, Brian, seemed to be steering the group and waived a paw so that 'Pauline' could speak uninterrupted.

'They're going after poor Cherie Bear again - see this picture they've found of her with the wind blowing her bonnet about, just as she's meeting that sawn-off frog from Florence, Silvio the Seducer? I wouldn't put it past her Tony to offer Cherie as part of some trade deal sweetener. They're all tarred wit' same brush. Wouldn't have him round my house.'

Brian came in quickly. 'Yes, isn't it interesting that there's little coverage of Tony Bear's policies, such as council cutbacks?'

'There's something in here,' said one of a pair of guinea pigs. 'Quite a good feature actually ...'

'They can keep going all morning on a good day,' said Boss as they moved on. 'Good way to forget yourself.'

Robert felt a warm regard for Boss at that moment; without him, the centre would have withered long ago. He and Ted Sloth must rally to the cause and if that meant rubbing shoulders with Bambino, then so be it.

Willie Mouse was tapping out an email and thinking about Rosealea's surprising news. How it might affect his temperamental team ... he could see she should have some maternity leave, but the prospects of Robert Bear acting the giddy goat in her absence while Ted Sloth discovered his radical roots made him wary. Thank goodness for the two German rookies, though this sat uneasily with him, being a long-suffering England fan. He thought of Otto's diligence and Lottie's legs. He put the email on hold and went next door to ask Manty, the bad-tempered Yorkie, if his special report was ready.

'Mant, is that draft of 'Steady as We Go' ready yet?'

'Give us a chance, man. Everybody's been crowding round here to look at this scan. Have a look, talk about going steady.'

Willie got another look at the inbred horror from the bottom of Woodville Lake and said he'd pop back in a bit. Outside, he bumped into Dr. Colera, the Irish Terrier, from adult general psychiatry. She'd heard the happy news and had some observations about genetic endowment and miscellaneous madnesses.

'Do your colleagues need some counselling about this? It's always best to know, you know.'

'I'm not so sure,' he replied and left 'Nutty Nora' at the top of the stairs, rolling on some smelly carpet.

SEVEN
WHO'S THAT LADY?

The fellows are made to visit the centre
Where love-lorn Ted claps eyes on a belter
She's from the new world and talks up a storm
If he wants to cop off, he'd best show some form.

WILLIE MOUSE DECIDED to do the decent thing. He could remember the thrill of it all when Maxine had been carrying their first - and last - half dozen. Now, their youngest had just left University. Robert had that to come; all too soon the parents' evenings, frosty wife and family Sundays.

He found Rosealea chatting to Henny Penny from the Early Intervention Team. 'Listen Rose, I don't think I should be setting you on with anything today. Is it right that you could pop next week? Do you want to go home?'

Henny gave him a look but agreed it might be a good idea. Rosealea set off home via her mother's to 'break the news before it's too late'.

Henny asked Willie to wait. 'We've been trying to do something with this young goat who believes he's Elvis ... keeps singing 'Cook Me Tender' and 'Like a Blessed Lamb'. Got a good voice actually.'

'Has he taken to eating ten burgers in one go?'

'No, but I think he'd benefit from the acceptance and therapeutic support I know is on offer at New Leaves Day Centre. They work wonders down there with some of our lot - such a valuable resource. Have I to contact Boss direct or go through you, Willie?'

'Send me an email.' He went back to his desk and switched off the computer.

What Rosealea wanted to do more than anything was find her dear Robby. She knew he was up to something important down at New Leaves and had laughed when he'd told her about Ted's involvement but now, she was all concern and anxiety. Whatever it was, *please let him be safe*. She knew she was being a bit girly and hormonal, a moment's reflection reassured her that any enterprise involving those two and Boss Grogan was going to be a one trick pony, unlikely to get out of first gear.

She caught the bus to her mother's and trusted Robert to tell his lot the big news as soon as he could. Old Ma Tamworth was busy pegging out a full basket when her daughter arrived. Rosealea was put off by this glimpse of woman's lot and knew she'd leave Robert if he ever put up a washing line. 'What on Earth are you doing, Mam?'

'Oh, hello, Chucky Egg - washers knackered again. Your father was fixing it, so I'll leave t'rest to your imagination. Husbands eh, don't you be in any hurry—'

'Mam, I'm pregnant.'

'Oh, darling, that's wonderful. Come here. How far gone are you?'

Mother and daughter fell into a damp clinch and the situation was explained.

Mother Pig found it all very amusing. 'Next week! Must be the Bear in her, keen to get her hands on some honey for tea. I remember when ...'

Rosealea wanted to sidestep the gynecological glossary of wonder her old Ma was happy to trot out at the smallest encouragement and asked after her dad. A retired fitter who ran a taxi.

'Out cabyin', so he says. Long as he's out from under my feet, shall I boil?'

All this reminded Rosealea why she'd left home in the first place - at 17, to live in a squat on Dead End Street. No wonder she became a social porker.

She found an uncluttered seat in the dingy kitchen. Was that what was in store for them? A flat earth version of Phillip Starling's awful poem ... get out as early as you can and don't have any pigs yourself? But they weren't having a pig, they were having a blind shot at a bright new whatever, who wouldn't have to face a cluttered kitchen or dreary hall. Robert could turn a capable hand to a knackered washer.

'We've no coffee, so it'll have to be tea.'

'Tea's fine, Mam.'

'It'll have to be powdered milk.'

'I'll take mine black.'

Ma mashed a pot of 'Nutbush' and moved some pots around the draining board. Rosealea's heart went out to her. Knocked up by her smooth-talking beau and saddled with six wieners in a rough council house before she could lay out her dreams. She wouldn't settle for that; no wonder she'd found a nice Bear from the other side of town.

'You and Robert Bear, eh? I saw his father at church the other week - handsome dude.'

'You what?'

'Good looking. Young Robert has a look of his Pa about him - nice.'

'I meant, when did you start going to church?'

'I didn't go in - I was selling a few pegs outside.'

'Tell me he didn't buy any.'

'No, he was too busy helping his wife get her own Mother through the door.'

'Look, Mam I've had my scan - here, what do you reckon?'

She looked at the image and burst into tears.

Boss Grogan had an idea for his visitors. 'How would you like to meet BIMBO, at least the informal management group ... ask them anything you like?'

'What's their connection with mental health, Boss?' asked Ted.

'Ask them.'

'Oh, come on,' said Robert. 'We don't want to be like sheep in there.'

'There's a pair of Teasdale's actually, hardy types. No, I'll tell you what it is Ted. Basically, it's to do with the ways in which women's experience of cultural pressure is perceived in terms of individual pathology. You know the form - mind your manners and don't hit on the lookers.'

He led them off to a side room and knocked on the door before opening it on a group of six, who all turned to smile at the visitors. Robert spotted the two North Country sheep with their black faces and spindle shanks. There were also two smooth terriers, a fellow bear and a leggy American bittern.

Ted had forgotten Boss' advice and plonked himself as near to her as he could with a bland grin. She seemed not to notice and drawled something to one of the little dogs. Robert said 'hi'.

Then the other dog introduced herself as Pippa and made space for him to sit down.

Boss smiled and left them to it. Robert thought they seemed friendly enough and felt sure they wouldn't get shouted at.

Pippa's friend, Dorcas, started things off. 'Boss says you can save the centre, that's brilliant.'

Ted had settled and was focusing on a poster which said: 'Learn to Love Women's Movement' over a beautiful image of Edwardian lady boxer dogs dancing together in a field. 'Well,' he said. 'I hope we can do our bit to change a few minds.'

'That's mighty fine,' responded the American beauty in what Robert thought was a lazy Texan drawl. 'Now, let's have some introductions here. I'm Dallas Verplank, visiting reader in gender studies at Woodville Poly.'

'Oh, er - I'm Ted Sloth.'

'Robert Bear.'

'Dorcas.'

'And Pippa.'

The Sheep turned out to be Paulo and Francesca. Then the other Bear asked Robert if he recognised her. He looked hard and caught a fleeting impression of a small boy who collected corporation bus tickets but decided it couldn't be.

But it was. 'Don't you recognise your niece, Wilbur, you silly old bear?'

'Not done up like that, I don't. Are you feeling all right? Besides, you can't be my niece - they're Sandy and Cindy. If you're our Wilbur, why are you wearing a dress and green lippy?'

'It's called 'Deep Meadow' if you must know, and the dress is styled by Miss Haversham.'

Robert was rattled and lapsed into his Redcar mode; the rest were all ears of various shapes. 'Aye, well, it's deep something you're in. Does Uncle Teddy know?'

ROBERT TRIES TO HELP

'That my lips are a Deep Meadow? It shouldn't surprise him - he knows I've had a sex change.'

Ted decided to step in. 'It is a lovely dress, and I can see why you chose that colour. Did you go to that place down the precinct at Woodville?'

'Thank you, Ted, and perhaps this serves to raise a few points about men and women, eh, cousin Robby?'

'Is that so?' asked a shaken relative. 'Enlighten us then.'

'I think it's about not everything being as it seems and that, beneath the surface, men and women are more alike than not. We can learn from this and ameliorate the current plague of gender rancour. So much of the bad stuff is culturally determined, it warps and distorts, pulling us all out of shape, driving us mad. We don't have to let it.'

Dallas was grinning. 'Darn right, Wilbur, and it's at vital sites like New Leaves where people under pressure are finding themselves, where we can rediscover ourselves. Gender issues are factors of mental ill health. You guys gotta go back and sock it to them.'

Robert had got over the shock and been impressed by what he'd heard from Wilbur. There were plenty of points he wanted clarity over though. 'What about men must bog off - it's in your slogan?'

Paula piped up. 'It's just a bit of fun. We wanted to call ourselves BIMBO and needed something to fit.'

'Things aren't always what they seem,' advised Dorcas.

'I'll make some tea,' said Dallas.

The visitors were beginning to feel a bit reconstructed, but could an American produce decent tea?

· · ·

After some small talk - Pippa turned out to be a footie fan - and after quite acceptable tea, the group got back onto weightier matters.

Francesca fished out some papers. 'I thought that following my presentation last week, we might continue along some similar pathways.'

Dorcas pushed a sheet of A4 in Robert's direction. He read that objects cast long shadows and passed it straight on to Ted, who had placed himself near Dallas again. Another sheet was more amusing. It showed a nice line drawing of a pair of guinea pigs in flagrante with a plate of chips and curry sauce placed in front of the female. She was trying hard to reach it as her mate pumped away with a look of distracted ennui. The line at the bottom was: 'had your chips today?'

Francesca wanted to hear what they made of the male guinea pig's expression. Wilbur thought constipated. Dorcas said stuck. Robert came up with grim determination.

Dallas was impressed. 'I guess you got him covered there, Robert, and your choice of words is very interesting, especially given that you're one of the fellows.'

'What about her?' asked Wilbur. 'She looks as if she's enjoying herself.'

'Yeah,' said Pippa. 'But what does she want most?'

Robert wondered why she couldn't have both. Ted sucked shamelessly up to Dallas, with some dubious stuff about the 'tyrannical urge' of the male sex drive and how often must women feel obliged to say yes when they really meant no. Or chips. Robert couldn't believe his chums' blathering and reflected that, if he went any further, he could kiss goodbye to chips with Miss Texas. It seemed to go down well in that quarter though.

'Listen, honey, that's just the sort of tune a broad likes to hear. You know, back home they've got this stuff you can mix in with a fellows' cornflakes ...'

And so on and so forth. Robert enjoyed the rest of the morning. The lasses were funny, so what if they daubed a building or two, it made you think. It seemed to him that Rosealea would be at home with the BIMBOS.

Following more input from Boss, Robert and Ted waited for the ferry back home and talked about their excellent adventure. They boarded with a group of school kids and sat at the front.

Robert was full of questions. 'You reckon you've pulled then mate?'

'I wouldn't put it like that.'

'Aye, I should box clever there if you're keen on her sexual policies.'

Ted let his stirred feelings show. 'Not as clever as whoever pulls your Wilbur.'

'Deck it, Dick'ed. You've no chance with Suzy Cream-cheese anyway - way out of your league. She was taking the piss. I know her sort; if you want your oats there, you'll have to negotiate every step along the way, then when you go off the boil, it'll be the crisis in masculinity. Right load o' cobblers.'

Ted remembered his chum's fling with a right-on Beaver from Welfare Rights a few years ago. Those wounds were still raw.

Robert was looking mulishly at the old lightning tree as they drifted past. They could see Ratty Rat on his boat by the riverbank. 'Look at him,' gestured Robert. 'Stupid prat, wants a good slap.'

'Why?' asked Ted. 'What's he ever done to you?'

'Oh, nothing. I dunno. It's this Wilbur business. He was a lovely little lad you know, used to sing for us all at family get-togethers. Like a little lark he was, then he grew up and got a job at the cake factory, where it all started, I should think.'

Ted decided to let his chum free associate till he'd had his say, then they joined the school kids listening to Auld Ned's tales of Pitcairn Island. As they approached the small pier at Woodville, Robert saw a familiar figure looking keenly in their direction.

Says Mother Bear 'it's all to do'
Obstetrics fates have favoured you
There's not much time left as we speak
You're going to be a father sometime this week.

'Eh,' said Robert. 'You what?'

'I'll be seeing you then, Robert. Bye Missus B,' said Ted as he sloped off.

'Yes, we need to put something together from this afternoon, don't we? See you, mate.'

Mrs. Bear knew Ted's mother at school and explained this to Robert. 'Yes, where is Rosy?'

'At ours. I'll drive us back and explain on the way.'

On the way across town, Robert heard about Rosealea's difficult day and the rapid developments. She was determined on a home birth too - Robert's mother's home.

'Hey, have a guess who I saw this afternoon?'

'Gaffer - he's been in trouble again, someone ought to do something.'

'No, not him, our Wilbur, Beattie's lad.'

Mother Bear pursed her lips and looked in the mirror. 'I heard something about him recently - been in some bother in a pub. Didn't sound like him.'

'Aye, well, this home birth ... she's never mentioned it before.'

'Well, as I say, all bets are off. It's some kind of wonder baby, a *she* by the way. Wait till you see the picture. She's smiling right back.'

He found this hard to take in. Next thing, the baby would be emerging with the power of speech and a set of school options.

'Oh, Robby, isn't it exciting?'

They turned into the road. Robert saw Mr. Pilling, the pongy old Airedale, from across the street, clipping his hedge, then his father looking anxiously from their garden gate.

EIGHT
A CHILD IS BORN

Our Robert needs to build a nest
For Mother, baby and the rest
There's carpets, curtains, baby stuff
But can he ever do enough?

ROBERT RAN from the car and called to his father. 'It's alright, son, she's in bed and her waters have started - I've sent for the midwife. I thought you were her. It's all happening faster than I remember. Where's your mother?'

Robert jerked his thumb backwards and ran up the stairs.

'In here,' called a familiar voice.

'This is my parents' room.'

'Yes, but even your dilatory dad could see how things were shaping up. Nice, isn't it?'

He was glad to hear that she was very much herself and asked to see 'this picture'. He was told to forget that as he'd soon be meeting the real thing.

'Have I to boil some water then?'

'No. Just sit down here.'

Robert took a front row seat by the bed, then Mrs. Bear cleared her throat on the landing. 'I've sent Teddy off to fetch your ma, Rosy, and the midwife is on her way. Isn't it exciting?'

Nothing else happened. Rosealea was content to lie still with her hands on her belly and Robert looked around a room he couldn't have spent more than a minute in since he was a child himself. The thought of the Prof's jam of changes and his parents early night made him smile, then a carefully framed picture on the wall made him fill up: a prize-winning water-colour he'd turned out at Sunday School, a charming but unlikely scene featuring the virgin, loosely based on Mrs. Bear, nursing a tightly swaddled cub with large ears.

'Babe Jeez' by Robt. Bear. He thought the child's face reminded him of something more recent, then Rosealea began to shift and fidget.

Robert decided she should be distracted. 'What a day. You would not believe what Ted Sloth and I found down at New Leaves - Boss Grogan's got it all to do.'

'Why, what's he on with now?'

'Smoker's corner, cake-making and sexual politics. That's just on a Tuesday - plenty of folk there mind. You ever heard of BIMBO?'

'Oo-oh, Robert. Do something, you great Herbert, don't just sit there like Soft Mick.'

'Rosy, is it coming? I'm sure they'll be here soon.'

She began to writhe so he ran downstairs. His mother was in the living room with her head in a cupboard. Overhead, something crashed and Rosealea cried 'bobbins'.

'I think she wants a bucket, Mam.'

'We'll not be needing anything like that. I'll go up to her, you go out to your father; he's standing around out there like a bunch of grapes.'

Mr. Bear was leaning on the gate with his back to the house, puffing his pipe and nattering with Sammy Fox from down the street. Robert overheard her saying that she might take after him for looks. Then his father saying, 'and for temperament I hope.'

'Dad, any sign of that nurse, and aren't you fetching Rose's lot?'

He looked down the street. 'Don't think so, son.'

'There must be something we can do,' urged Robert.

The Fox announced that all would be well, and all would be well and all would be well. This got Robert's dander up; she'd always been a meddlesome Mary and he was about to ask her what she was on about when the dirty old Terrier from across the road ambled over.

Robert went back in. Upstairs, his mother was stroking Rosealea's head and crooning 'Hands Across the Table' while Rosy moaned. He knew she'd never forgive him.

Ted was looking forward to that evening's broadcast of 'Botheration Street', the popular show based on the fantastic notion that humans could converse, make relationships and pursue gainful employment in shops and factories. It was set in cartoon form and very much enjoyed by higher functioning types. It wouldn't be on for another hour, so he decided to start clarifying his day centre thoughts while they were still fresh.

He took up a pose of settled contemplation at the table by the window and opened a fresh pad of A4. He recalled her lovely long legs, kissy lips and saucer eyes, the way she wore her hair like the braid of a minimalist fez. The sock it to 'em assertiveness and passion for the liberating potential of social care. It all flowed from this. The centre was steeped in the values of enablement and empowerment - involvement and self-determination too, not to mention user participatory initiatives, no end of those.

Boss Grogan had shown them that it could all be costed out to a sustainable model, nay, a cost-saving paradigm because people stayed better for longer and thus reduced demands on other areas of the service. The New Leaves group's work enabled troubled souls to share their pain and transform their experience in a therapeutic setting. Finally, something was beginning to bloom on these new branches of recovery. An elegant example of the social model of mental strain, a women's group challenging the roles and pressures that might send them distracted. Ted tarted it up a bit with some more smart welfare talk, shamelessly trumpeting the certainty of 'savings to be made' if the centre stayed open and they could 'realign' the Crisis Team and 'rationalise' community treatment services. Ted had always known he had it in him and now he had his chance.

'Deep breaths,' said Mrs. Bear.

'What happens now, Mum?'

'It ought to be straightforward from this point. The little lovey wants to get here, there's no doubting that.'

'Little lovey, little - you're havin' a right ... 'uckin' 'ell. She must be ... ohhhh.'

'That's right, Rosy, duck you let rip it'll loosen you up and speed things along.'

'Sweaty arse-ole furrk ... come on, you little sod.'

Mr. Bear knocked on the door with Banty the midwife. 'Well,' she said. 'You've started without me. Not far off, if I'm any judge.'

'I hope you are,' said Rosealea with feeling.

Robert moved up to the top of the bed to hold her hot little trotter. He held his breath when Banty asked Rosealea to talk to him, but all she could manage were some compound adjectives and an attack on the bedhead with her free arm. Banty told her that was good, and she was doing fine.

'Mr. Bear, have you got some sturdy gardener's twine and a strong hook?'

He looked at his wife in confusion; she told him the midwife simply wanted to rig up some stirrups. He pottered off on his mission and soon came back with the goods.

Banty took charge and as soon as Mr. Bear had screwed his hook into the ceiling, Rosealea was told to cast aside her quilt and push. Then it all happened.

The most amazing thing Robert had seen since the old Professor had made an Elephant fly, but better. The sturdy twine held as Rose began to thrash and wail, then a little head appeared then - with a short flush, the rest of the baby. The new mother tried to look but it was difficult for her to see from where she was.

'Cut her down now, please,' requested Banty, then she set to work with sheets and a bowl, at one point blowing carefully into the child's mouth.

Then there was a soft gurgle - Rosealea was holding the baby and Robert caught his head on the wardrobe on his way to the cold lino.

Ted had turned off the tele and played with more phrases to challenge the centre's closure: - 'politically otiose', 'a really bad idea', 'talk about crackers'- before flipping through a pile of CDs stacked by his smart little player. He lingered over 'Dig It' by Miff Mole and his Molers but settled on 'Hootin'' by Nat

Towells and his Night Owls. This being 'classic jazz from Burton on Trent', a little-known hotbed of Dixieland Jazz. As far as Ted was concerned, it was the perfect antidote to awkward colleagues and uppity women; he always knew where he was with Miff and Nat.

'Wake up, son, you're missing all the fun.'

'What's happening?' Robert looked around and found he was lying next to Rosy on his parent's big double bed. 'Where's the baby?'

'Just over her,' said Banty, who was giving her the once over. 'Lovely little lass - thought of a name yet?'

'Dallas - I mean little lass - we've had a girl.'

'I told you it was going to be a girl. We thought Phoebe - now come 'ere and meet your dad.'

Robert sat up and steadied himself against the undamaged headboard and held his arms out stiffly. He was told to relax. When he finally got to hold her, he was entranced. She looked just like the baby in an old tapestry; she gazed at him and smiled as he cradled her.

'That's just wind, I'm afraid,' said Banty.

'Isn't she supposed to be a forward child though?'

'Of course she is,' answered Rosealea. 'I'm sure there was a grin in there as well.'

Downstairs, Mr. Bear was mashing tea and talking to his pal at the back door.

'What's he want now?' asked his wife as he took her cup through. 'Always on the scrounge and he smells. Tell him he's welcome to a bath if he wants.'

'Does he live on his own?' inquired Banty.

'Yes. I suppose I ought to be more neighbourly. His Queenie passed last year - caught kennel cough, then it turned to swine flu, and she was a goner. Still, life goes on.'

'It certainly does. You know the hospital will be taking a special interest in Phoebe, don't you?'

'No,' replied Banty. 'But she's ... noteworthy. The races intermingle all the time, of course. My own great-grandmother on my father's side was a stormy petrel - there are times when I feel the call of the sea myself ...'

Mrs. Bear thought she'd offer to take her there if she didn't get to the point. 'What gives with our little Phoebe?'

'The children of bears and pigs together are extremely rare and it's a long time since it happened round here. With our modern ways, we can discover things about some of the more mysterious aspects of life today.'

'But why? Robert and Rosealea seem to click right enough ... she's got a sharp tongue mind and he can be a bit mardy ... but they're obviously making hay.'

'I find most of it a bit over my head, but Phoebe may help us to make better babies.'

'You should be studying our Robert then - seems to have the right stuff. We could hire him out.'

Banty was keen to go. Her job sometimes brought her up against the quixotic and careless ways in which nature scattered its bounty. She looked over Mrs. Bear's shoulder to see small clouds of cigar smoke and catch the sounds of cautious male laughter. 'I must be off. Listen, what we do know is that such babies have remarkable growth rate in the early months; in fact, from the very beginning, you've seen how fast the pregnancy's been. It should slow down by the second month, by which time she'll be walking, talking, and saying no.'

'Teddy, you may as well bring your friend in. It seems our little sweetie-pie's some sort of genius.'

'This is my chum, Robert, and this is Banty, the midwife.'

'Here, ragged tash, you sit by the table,' said Mrs. Bear, but she couldn't help smiling as the old Dog sat next to Banty with his great tongue lolling.

'Right,' said Banty. 'I'm off.'

Mrs. Bear spent another ten minutes thanking her on the doorstep, then the put-upon health worker escaped.

'I'm sure she's laughing at me,' said Robert.

'Soft Herbert, it's wind. The midwife told you. Thank God she was here though, it all happened so fast. She came out like a rocket, Robert. I thought she would fly through the window - Banty really did have to catch her. She left some cream. I'm as sore as owt. Never am I having sex again. I've done my bit.'

He looked in the pile of baby stuff and found a jar marked 'Ladies Balm'. Rosy slapped some on and it did the trick. He looked at Phoebe in her makeshift crib. She seemed settled on her back, watching the light play about the ceilings fading paper. She was very absorbed, and Robert was able to inspect her from the waist down. He thought she resembled a guinea pig with a lovely pink belly and tiny little trotters; she also had a curly tail. There was something wrong though: she was too contented. He felt that wouldn't last, her being a child of Rosealea's.

'What happens next, Rosy? Will she want a feed or rocking, or something? I don't have much of a clue, to be honest.'

'Join the club, Father Bear.'

He just about managed to stop himself saying something along the lines of women knowing about these things. 'She's lovely though, isn't she, just like in those tapestries of sacking? In a way, it was foretold wasn't it ...'

'Robert, you've had a long day. You lie down for a bit while I mix up some of Banty's powders.'

He had another look before his rest. She turned her perfect head to him and smiled, definitely. She also murmured something that could almost have been 'Erbert', but as Rosy said, it had been a long one. How had they brought all this about?

Rosealea lay back on the bed with Robert. She thought it would be good if the three of them could stay for a while in the Bears' back bedroom. Just a couple of weeks to be looked after and given time. Her thoughts began to drift as the curtains of fretfulness became drifting Poplars, the chest of drawers a man's jolly face. Then she was pulled back sharply to the moment by cross sounds in the street: a sudden banging of a car door, then a termagant's wail. 'You said you'd fixed it.'

'Shut up, you don't know how knackered it was.'

'Neither did you, Soft Walter.'

Her parents had arrived and Mr. Bear was already outside, offering to help with the car. For a while, down below, the sounds came and went as the men talked of overheated engine heads. If her mother joined in they'd be there all night, but she was soon bustling up the stairs with Mrs. Bear.

'Ooh,' she cooed. 'Just look at her.'

Phoebe looked at her and said 'Erbert'.

Robert was stirred the next morning by a nursery chorus of 'lerbelerbelerbel Lerbelergul lerbelerbut'. He was determined to start as he meant to go on and got up to see to the baby so Rosy could rest a bit longer.

'Ello darlin'... 'ello Daddy's little sweetie-pie.'

She gazed blankly in his direction and said 'Herbert'. This time there was no ambiguity.

He chuckled fondly and reached down to lift out his damp

and whiffy treasure. He had a fair grasp of what was required and soon had her cleaned, creamed and nappied. He put her back into the cot where she lerbelled away for a bit.

Then Rosealea came to, in some pain. 'Where's that effin cream - Jesus wept.'

'Here,' he said, waving the jar of baby balm.

'Not that, you Herbert - that fanny cream Banty left. It's got pink flowers on the label.'

He found the 'Soft Lips Lotion' and tossed it across, then took a sudden interest in the street. There was a clear patch of oil on the road in front of the house and a pair of rabbits were fighting on their way to school.

Rosealea called him back and told him that he 'had a big job on today'.

'How do you mean?'

'Nest building.'

'Come again?'

'Listen, you'll have to move in at mine, so I want you to make ready. I'll write it down.'

As far as he could see, when the list was ready, there was a lot of lifting and shifting and then plenty of cleaning. There was also a subsection which involved a trip to Motherbare. Robert could already see problems. His father had offered to drive him and generally lend a hand. Mrs. Tamworth was due to call again, so he was happy to help. Mr. Pilling appeared as they got the car out and cadged a lift 'uptown'.

'Busy day?' asked Mr. Bear.

'Bit of business down Basketgate, then a spot of lunch with our St. John. Might take in a film later at the Arts Lab.'

'Nice old dog,' said Robert after they'd dropped him off outside British Worm Stores. 'Seems to fill up his day.'

'Mmm,' said Mr. Bear. 'I thought his St. John was working

on an oil rig ... never one for lunch dates with his dad, as I remember. Any way best get it over with, eh?'

They parked up and went straight to Motherbare, where helpful women found his requirements and suggested others, even Rosealea, had overlooked. Robert couldn't believe how much it all cost and wanted a pint after they'd loaded up the car.

'Plenty of time to wet the baby's head, son - have you told them at work what's going on?'

'They knew Rosy was expecting.'

'Maybe so, but no one was expecting what happened. I'll drop you off up there, then head for Rosy's, if you give me the key.'

'Oh, erm ... yes, right. Good idea.'

'You've had a shock, lad. It's all change now.'

NINE
THE VISION THING

Our Robert's life has altered utterly
With child and wife, more responsibility
To change the ways of a carefree bear
And freight his days with wear and tear.

ROBERT'S HEAD might have been spinning but the well-ordered life of Woodvilleshire County Council was going on just the same. As he approached the large revolving doors, he remembered that the place was like a big church. He lingered in awkward reverence, then slid through to reception, using up some more time admiring the portraits in oils hanging in dim corporation light around the walls. There were no bears, but he did find a pig - Alderman Mango, who saw through the modernisation of the Towns drainage system in 1904.

He went upstairs to the social work department. There was no one about, then Ted appeared with some papers. 'Hi there, Robert, what happened to you?

'Rosy's had her baby - my mam came to collect me. It all happened very quickly. She's called Phoebe.'

Ted hesitated. 'What a lovely name. Are you coming in? I think Willie's here somewhere.'

'Yeah, what are you on with?'

'That day centre stuff - I got started last night. I could do with running some of it past you.'

'I don't know as I've time ...'

A door opened and Willie Mouse poked his head into the corridor. 'Here he is, congraters Robert, the midwife's told me all about it. Come in; you too, Ted. We'll wet the baby's head.'

'I should get back, Rosy wants ...'

'Never mind what Rosy wants. He'll have plenty of time for that, eh, Ted?'

Ted gave his chum a don't-blame-me look and smiled blandly at their suddenly playful manager. Was he pissed? Had he succumbed to late onset heebie-jeebs?

Willie closed the office door behind them and struggled beneath his desk to produce a four-pack of 'Nutt's Nectar'. 'A left over from last Christmas. Uncle Willie's winter warmer, keeps out the cold at six per cent.'

'Maybe you just don't care after a glass or two,' suggested Ted, who was now keen to get his hands on some.

Willie pulled the rings on three tins and handed them round. 'Here's to Robert and family - first of many, eh?'

The new father took a long sip to evade that one. It didn't matter; jovial Willie was in the chair and the wind had caught his sails. 'This reminds me of when I first qualified and old Tom Cat took me for a lunchtime session ...'

Robert's dad had been shocked by the spartan quality of Rosealea's home. He'd anticipated signs of a woman's touch, but it was all so sparse and spare. Robert had been used to soft furnishings and thick rugs, central heating, polished mahogany.

Rosy had no carpets and the curtains looked on the thin side. He thought Robert must be very much in love to fall in with a tribe of porkers and such-like. He was still feeling the impact of her parents' visit with the cylinder head from hell. The old boy had actually thanked him for 'taking our Rose on'.

He found the upstairs to be a bit better, with cork boards in the bathroom and smartly made-up beds, though he looked in vain for a pine ottoman and upstairs telly. He felt for the poor lass and wanted to brighten the place for her homecoming. He decided to go round to Robert's - combining their households was the answer. He knew that his son had an ironing board.

Banty had called round to the Bears to see how mother and baby were doing. She found Phoebe sucking at her 'titty bottle' (at roughly the same time as her father was sipping his 'Nectar' at County Hall). But Rosealea was in a flat and despondent mood in the living room, a folk museum tableau of post war home comfort. Mrs. Bear poked her head through a serving hatch to ask who wanted tea.

Rosealea began to cry. 'I want to go home; this place gives me the creeps. It's like an episode of Miss Marsupial investigates. Phoebe doesn't need me.'

'That'll change soon,' Banty assured her. 'Where's Robert?'

'Him and his dad are sorting out the house - my house - for us.'

'You're bound to feel differently when the three of you are together.'

This led to some wailing in earnest. 'But that's just it - living with Robert. He can be such a numpty and I've been round his place ... it's just like here. Ducks on the wall, smelly old armchairs. That's all he is ... a smelly old couch. How are we all going to live together?'

Banty embraced the frazzled mum and after some restorative sharing of women's wisdom, Rosealea's mood began to lighten. Then Phoebe called 'Ierbert'.

'Let's have a look at her,' said Banty.

Phoebe seemed to enjoy being inspected as she lay on her back, trying to catch hold of her tail with her little feet. Mrs. Bear came in with the tea and observed that wasn't she lovely.

'Anyway, Ted, have you told Willie about our trip down river and the remarkable things we saw with Boss Grogan?'

'Oh, I've heard all about it,' said Willie Mouse.

'Not really *all* of it,' stated Ted.

'There's more then.'

Ted waived some sheets of A4 like important papers and told them he'd already 'formulated some interesting trackers for service development'. Did they want to have a look? Details were distributed. 'You'll see that I've collated my perceptions in a five-point plan.'

'That's two used up already,' said Willie as he winked at Robert.

'Yes, anyway P also means persuasion and I intend my process to do just that.'

'Go on then,' said Willie as he lit up a cigar.

'Right,' nodded Ted. 'It boils down to persuasion, partnership and participation - thus paving the way to praxis.'

'Is that further down river from New Leaves then?'

'You what?'

'Well,' said Willie, perhaps seriously. 'I thought that could be a name for your study - paving the way to praxis. Got a nice ring to it. Like Working my Way back to You Babe. Who else is in on it with you?'

'Robert is but he's going to be busy at home now, so I want

to pursue some academic partnership - via a contact I made when we were there.'

Robert tuned in. 'Who was that then?'

'You remember Dallas, that visiting American? She's got some interesting ideas. I've got her number.'

Pa Bear thought he was in an episode of 'Location Location' with Kirsty Chick. It was a favourite of his but the programme he really liked was that one where they did your house up while you're out. Such a kind thing to do for someone, a bit of a surprise like, but they generally got their bearings. He chuckled as he unloaded more of Robert's gear. It'd be a present to the three of them. A home should reflect everyone who lived there he thought as he fixed his son's framed poster of Captain Barmpot and the Tragic Band above the fireplace. With those boxes of CDs at hand, he could entertain little Phoebe. He turned his attention to the bare floorboards.

Back at the Bears' place, Rosealea was still keen to get home. 'No offence, Mrs. B you've been brilliant, but I just want to return to familiar surroundings, my nice little house. I can't expect you to put me up for much longer anyway.'

'Oh, I understand love, I'd be the same. There really is no place like home, as the song goes: be it ever sooo 'umble there's nooo place ....'

'Have I to come with you?' asked Banty.

'Would you?'

'Corse. I just need to nip over to County Hall, then I'll come straight back.'

. . .

'You might have her number, but has she got *yours?*' Willie asked Ted waggishly.

'Darn right Ted, spot on,' said Robert.

'Yeah,' said Ted. 'She said that, and she also told me that gender relations are a key site for mental health. We should lay it on y'all, or something.'

'Will it mean you have to talk like an American sloth?' asked Willie.

The lunch-time drink had made Ted a bit testy. 'Look, it's all in here if you want to read it. I can't help my passion. I've got a vision.'

'Another *pea* then?' asked Robert.

Ted told him he should be at home.

Willie didn't want his lads falling out and asked Ted to give him a rough outline.

'There's nowt wrong with a bit of passion. I had some of it once, but it didn't really suit me.'

Ted swallowed the last of his drink in a mannish way and wiped his mouth with the back of a paw. 'My vision - and I think Boss is on board with this - is to rebrand New Leaves as a more inclusive person-centered centre, centering round radical views of mental health and recovery. It'll be underpinned by normalisation and expanding definitions of stuff so that mental ill health becomes a normal part of life. As such.'

Robert couldn't believe what he was hearing but their manager seemed impressed. 'Sounds just the job, but where does this Denver lass fit in?'

'It was her that gave me the vision. I was summarising the social models of mental suffering and she agreed and said that places like New Leaves should be forcing houses for reconstruction and social healing. I saw a beautiful mind in front of me.'

Robert was scornful. 'He fancies her, within the parameters of the social model of course.'

Willie was interested. 'This sounds potentially very interesting. Have a word with your cutie-pie from Colorado and put something together. I'll take it to committee next week, should liven things up. What do you think Robert? Some of these ideas are yours, I take it?'

'I was present, but Ted's done the leg work, the way he's presented it is ... remarkable, really.'

'Yes,' said Willie. 'Just so, now I'm going to contact Grogan - you might want to connect with Dallas, Ted.'

They sat for a while after he'd gone, then Ted spoke. 'If we can lay on some 'Nectar' for next week's committee, Willie might talk it through without too much trouble.'

Robert decided he needed some fresh air.

He went out by the rear of the building and found Banty smoking a cigarette. He told her he didn't know she smoked.

'I didn't know you drank at work.'

'Just to wet the baby's head.'

'Aren't you meant to be sorting out the house, ready for baby's return?'

'Yeah, on with it now.'

'Right, so what are you gathering for the nest? Some rubber bands, paper clips? This baby's a quick learner, maybe she'd like to read last year's under-fives provision report.'

Alright fagash, he thought, *they'll be cutting your lot next.* 'Right, well. I'd best be making tracks.'

'You can't drink and fly.'

'No, I guess not.' Why did they ask so many questions? It was obvious he'd disgraced himself. It was slow torture. Maybe it was what gallus Dallas meant by 'the grinding attrition of gender rancour'.

Banty seemed to sense this. 'I'm on my way back to your parents to take Rosealea and little Phoebe back to hers. I think her mother is meant to be coming across too. Shall I drop you off on the way?'

'Would you mind?'

'I think it'll be for the best, don't you?'

Her smart Pterodactyl was waiting in the car park, snorting at a couple of cherubs who had climbed on his back uninvited. 'Naff off, yer little 'orrors, 'shouted Banty. 'I knew you when you were babes.' She petted 'Terry', who could be temperamental but loyal and friendly once he knew you.

Robert gave him a fond tickle under the chin before settling himself comfortably on the mighty beast. They were soon airborne from practically a standing start. He remembered the flight back from Redcar, Rosey's pink ears catching the wind like socks on a washing line. It wasn't far to her house and as Terry took them down, he could pick out the back garden. As they flew nearer, he recognised his father among some furniture on the lawn.

Terry set them down and Banty said she'd be back soon 'with the others'. Then he took off and was soon a flapping shape in the lower sky.

'Grand types, they are,' said Mr. Bear. 'Treat 'em right and you've a friend for life.'

'Dad what's all this doing out here? They'll be here in a minute.'

'Ah, right ... well, I thought the place seemed a bit cheerless. Not somewhere you'd want to bring a baby back to. I think that, like a good marriage, a happy home should combine the best of two worlds. Go and see, I'm jiggered now.'

Robert saw that he should show some appreciation and managed a tepid 'Ta Dad' as he crossed the back doorstep.

The kitchen didn't look too bad with a few of his mugs and a retro railway poster he was sure she wouldn't mind. The hallway was a different story; the last time he'd been there, it had been a welcoming light-filled space. A cane chair stood by the door opening onto striped pine sparseness, which had been converted into a furniture warehouse. There was another chair, which didn't match, his old trunk, character hat stand, rug and, horror of horrors, another randomly tacked poster, of Tony Bear, the celebrated illusionist. Why had he kept that? He wished the plausible trickster was there now to smooth things over.

He couldn't look anywhere else and went outside to tell his father that Rosy didn't like a lot of clutter.

'I could see that when I came over this morning. You can't bring t'little lass home to an empty house. Besides, you've got some decent sticks of furniture. It was like a vision I had. It all goes well together, don't you think? I've done my back in though; wouldn't want to do it again.'

Robert wondered if his old pa had been on the Professor's jam again. The aging egghead had caused more trouble than enough, one way and another; next time he went mad, they should get him on a Home Office restriction order. As these shadows played across his troubled mind, a dot dilated in the sky.

'Here they come, lad - bye she takes no time at all on that great serpent. See him use his tail to steer them.'

Robert's beer-soaked euphoria had morphed into clinical anxiety. He joined Mr. Bear to wave a welcome. As they landed, he saw that Rosealea was very pale and Banty was

125

holding the baby. He heard her telling Rosy that she would soon feel a lot better

in familiar surroundings.

'Hi babe, how are you?' She told him to shush and handed Phoebe over in her basket. 'I've ordered Rose to go straight for a lie down. She's exhausted and must have as much rest as possible.'

'Don't you worry on that account, sister,' said Mr. Bear. 'She'll be happy in her bower of bliss.'

Rosealea went into the kitchen and Banty gave Robert a look.

'Where's all this shit come from?' was heard from the back door, then she went into the hall. 'I'll kill 'im.'

As she stormed back into the garden, Robert held the basket close, reasoning that she'd be less likely to assault him holding the baby. Banty stood closer to Mr. Bear, who obviously thought Rosealea was about to clock one of them. He could see that his big surprise had been a bad idea.

She drew a deep breath. 'This is down to you two, isn't it? You pair of Herberts, what were you thinking of and where's all that gear from Motherbare?'

'That'll still be in the boot,' replied Mr. Bear.

Phoebe had woken up and looked up at her father. 'Erbert erbert lerbul luh.'

'She really is a quick learner,' snorted Rosealea.

'You know,' he said. 'I'm sure she's called me that before.'

'Erbert erbut,' she trilled and kicked her trotters.

'She'll like it in there,' he said. 'We've set up lots of interesting nooks and hidey holes.'

Mother was unimpressed. 'Nooks and holes, there's no way I'm taking her in there. Done a risk assessment have you?'

Banty moved down the garden path. 'I'll be heading off then.'

'No don't, Bant,' said Rosealea as she scooped up baby and basket. 'I want to go to that place you were telling me about.'

'What's she giving it now?' asked Robert, bemused. 'What have you been telling her?'

'It's a new place for women in unsafe domestic situations - part of a project piloted by the Women's Studies Centre. There's an American lass called Phyllis—'

'Isn't she called Dallas?' asked Robert.

'Yes, you know her then?'

'In a way. Why do you want to go there, babe?'

'Give you two wazzocks a chance to sort out this unsafe situation that I need rescuing from.'

'Well, I'm jiggered,' murmured Robert's father.

'But what about Phoebe?' Robert wanted to know.

'What about her? I'm not leaving her with you.'

As Banty and Rosealea went down towards Terry, Robert heard a small precious sound. Phoebe was saying 'wazzock'.

TEN
SEXUAL POLITICS

Poor Robert and family are parted
He feels fed up and misjudged
Our hero tries but can't get started
As his best schemes come out fudged.

TED SLOTH COULDN'T BELIEVE his luck. It was all going his way - his manager had given him a free hand with the day centre project, he'd found a brilliant 'Jimmy Pug' cardigan at Woodville's finest tat shop. And he was on his way to meet drop-dead Dallas, the fittest bird he'd seen for ages. Possibly ever.

'Heard about Rosie?' called Lucy Beaver as he untethered his bike at County Hall.

'Yeah, brilliant, isn't it?' he shouted as he sped off. He didn't hear the affronted Beaver call him a jerk.

Lottie asked what was troubling her.

'They're all t'same, think everything's a laugh. Only funny thing with that one's his cardie - what a twit.'

· · ·

Ted's journey took him through the town and past a crowd, clapping and singing. He asked a baby elephant in a kilt what was happening. It was a raucous response to the proposed council cuts. He parked up and joined in an uncertain rendition of 'Dancing Queen', which reminded him of Alan Partridge off the telly. Carried up with the revolutionary fervor, he sang 'Aha at County Hall wicked Tories did surrender' but it didn't seem to fit. Then he saw a rough cairn terrier with eggs in a box and decided he'd done enough on the frontline. Looking back, the council building looked grim and sturdy with the protestors gathered in uncertain light, like a shoal of guileless fish. He didn't want to be there when the trawlers rolled in.

Compared to the classical utility of County Hall, Woodville University was a drab spot - flat-roofed and grey, with green mould seeping between the pre-cast slabs. Lots of litter and streaked windows. There were a few students wandering with purpose, but they looked a thin and sallow lot - the lasses lank and sexless, the lads tatty and spavined. A pair of rabbits lolloped past as he locked up his bike. One of them dropped a lit cigarette and the other said 'pubs'll be open'. He wondered what use a bad degree would be to a dilatory lop ear. When he and Robert had done their social work diplomas at Open Air College, it had been difficult; they'd had to work a bit, not like this lot getting it all on a plate after what passed for 'A' levels today. If he could retake his now ...

'Hey there, sweet cakes, come right on up - room 101.'

Ted's bad mood dispersed like breath from the kind of stained window that Dallas was calling from.

'Right,' he said. 'I'm on my way.'

As he moved towards the building, he could hear comments from the open window - 'and so cute', 'has he got a friend'? Did this mean he was in a yellow wood on a road what sit travelled - less, was it? Should he turn back and get on his bike, or climb the sticky stairs of destiny? In the end, it was a no brainer, and what was that other one he tried to remember - a doozy? He reckoned he should just be himself. It was what Dallas seemed to like.

She met him on the stairs. 'Hey there, Ted, good to see ya. I got something I just know you're gonna go for.'

'But it's never not right, Robby, the lass must be puddled - used to happen in my day. They'd got some daft idea into their heads, then before you could say Dr. Doolittle, the babes would be in waifs home cots and there'd be nowt on your table when you got home. You'd have the devil of a job gettin' 'em back. Ask your mother ... what was the name of that donkey in Mudd Street who took a left turn? Persephone or Andromeda – Donna! That was it. Well, she ...'

Robert's Granny had visited to meet her new great-grand-daughter and ended up giving advice to her troubled grandson. His dad reckoned she meant well but Robert had taken firmly against her when she left him out in the rain as a child. He wished she'd bog off. 'Mum, things are different now. This place is charged with helping families stay together, not separate.'

Granny wasn't persuaded. 'I dare say that's what they've told you.' She stuck a sweet in her mouth and closed her eyes.

His mum shook her head and rolled her eyes in Granny's direction. The grandson picked up a handy bread knife and made melodramatic *Psycho* gestures behind the old woman.

'Joe's Garage,' he said.

'What?' asked his mother.

'The name of this puddled partner's place. I bet Ted Sloth's

American beauty has something to do with it as well. Honestly, poking her sticky beak in, giving advice where it's not wanted, thank you very much ...'

'You'll be talking yourself out of a job at this rate,' said Granny without opening her eyes.

'Well, be that as it may, Mum, it does seem as if she's had bad advice from somewhere. Have you been able to talk to Rosy, pet, or see the baby?'

'Oh I've been given guidance and wise counsel. Banty came back when Dad and I were trying to get things straightened up. That overgrown newt she gets about on left us something too, right by the back door. More for me to clear up before they'll consider coming back.'

'Isn't that Banty good though - goes the extra mile every time,' said his mother.

'If you say so ... you know it was her that told Rosy about this safe place for troubled ladies.'

'Well, I dare say she was only trying to help. Mother generally knows best.'

Granny nodded and cracked her mint.

Robert steeled himself. 'Dad was only trying to help; it's not as if I'd dropped the baby or bashed Rosy.'

'Oh, you don't want to be going in for that, our Robert, no wonder the lass has taken the way she has. You'll be needing a place of safety when her family finds out - never thought a grandson of mine would lift his hand to a lady.'

'Mam, what about a nice glass of port? You could have it outside with a smoke, eh?'

'Yes, sun's got out again - give me a chance to talk some sense into your brute of a son.'

After she'd been maneuvered into the backyard, Robert told his mother that Gran should be grateful he was a non-violent bear.

131

'She'll have forgotten it all after a few Sandemans. Why don't you take her one out?'

As he took her the port and the papers, she winked at him and said she knew he'd never be a granny-basher. He laughed at the old bat and remembered how much he loved his Nana Bear, even though he'd never understood her - or any woman properly, not even his mum, and as for Rosy and little Phoebe.

Ted Sloth was running in fast company.

'Robert,' called his mother. 'Will you go over to help your dad? He was worn out last night.'

Ted was shuffling through his second lot of papers, having passed the first lot back to Dallas. She'd been studying them quietly for a while, giving him a chance to look around the office. She shared it with Ingrid, a research terrier, who was stuck to her computer screen. Dallas explained later that the brainy little dog was part of a fascinating project, looking at ways to stem the diminishment of humans. Also, studying them was good in other ways as they too were part of the bio-system, and findings could throw up valuable clues for higher functioning life systems. He remembered some of the sightings by the settlements near New Leaves. Would anyone really miss them if they were simply allowed to die out?

'Darn tootin', Teddy boy.'

'Eh?'

'Your ideas, Ted – lickety-split and moving nicely.'

'Yes ... yes, well, they're just outline proposals, but I think the basic theme of inclusion is quite evident, and with the recovery model underpinning a strong commitment to reciprocity, the value base is sound.'

Dallas turned to Ingrid. 'Get a load of this jive. These British welfare cats can sure shoot the breeze. Now, honey, run it past me one more time; a girl gets dazzled by too much moonshine.'

Ingrid had spun round in her chair so that the pair of them were facing him expectantly. 'Well, sans moonshine, if we can get enough people into the day centre and get them to keep coming till they start feeling better, with the groups and all that, then we'll be in a good - a reciprocal - way of business. Now, I've been thinking about your ideas of what bothers us. It correlates with some perspectives from the social model of disability where relational capital ...'

'Ted, honey, aim all that fancy stuff; the first bit was just fine.'

'Sounds interesting,' said Ingrid as she turned back to her computer screen.

Robert's mind was wandering and wondering as he made his way to Rosealea's place via the old bicycle works on Tatters Fields. The place held sentimental capital for him as it was the site of his earliest sexual experiences with Fiona, an enthusiastic badger, from school. They had gone out properly for a while, till she'd come round one night to listen to records. He'd put on The Groundhogs and moved in for a snog, but she'd kicked up at the 'weirdo music' and called him a 'stupid 'ippy'. And that had been that, out of the blue, no sense to it. They were all a sodding mystery. He looked in on the abandoned office where love had first hovered and wondered what might have happened to his sixth form sex bomb. Had she left the area? Was she working for the council? Had she really cared for him, at all?

'Can I help you?'

He turned to see a goat in a scruffy blue uniform. 'Only it's private property this and you're trespassing.'

'I've been coming here for years since I was a cub. In fact when I was seventeen I ...'

'Yes, I dare say, but it's unsafe - coming down properly next week for a new branch of Wilkos.'

'Oh, well, this is the way we live now, I suppose. Mind if I cut across the back way?'

'Oh, you're alright, but think on, eh?'

By the time he got to Rosealea's, Robert had a better grasp of the issues and how to win back his flighty partner. Father and son would pull together to recreate her bower of whatever it was she called it. The memory of Fiona and the 'ippy music had clarified that it didn't do to impose your tastes just like that.

He found his father fast asleep in one of the armchairs that would probably need shifting. He looked knackered and Robert felt bad. It stirred up another shard of lost time for him. He must have been seven, his go cart wouldn't go, and he'd thrown a wobbler. His dad had spent the best part of his Sunday afternoon in the shed with it till it 'went like the clappers'.

He began to fill up and moved into the hall. He was met by the poster of Tony Bear - so much of life was dealing with disappointment. He looked at the disgraced magician and said, 'slick twat'.

'Eh, who's that?'

'Who were you talking to - sounded like a row?'

'Tony Bear, he's a soft twit.'

'Oh.'

'Hey, Dad, have you heard the latest?'

'Eh?'

'They're going to pave paradise and put up a new branch of Wilkos.'

'Aye, over by the old bike works him from over the road was

saying. Reckons they might take him on - meet and greet, that'd be a laugh.'

'Isn't he a bit ...?'

'Clapped out? Yes, but his mind's still sharp. They'll want someone to count the nails.'

'He'll have to cancel those lunches with St. John?'

Robert was playing for time and was ready to spin an extended tale of Nana Bear before he decided his dad deserved better. 'Listen, Dad, I'm really sorry about all this but I've had a good idea.'

'Oh, aye?'

'It's simple really. I'll phone for a van and ask for an extra pair of hands. Also, it'll force me to chuck some of my stuff. High time really.'

'You sure, son?'

'Say, Ted, let's you and me go over to Joe's. I can show you around and we can do lunch.'

'Won't they mind me being a ... dude?'

Dallas chortled and rested a wing on his lumpen shoulder. 'I'll vouch for you; you're a very fine old English gentleman, with some exciting policy potential.'

He was sure Dallas had just made physical contact with him for significantly longer than might have been expected. He tried to come up with more cute things to say as they walked across the campus. Unfortunately, a colleague of Dallas' - a prattling pine martin called Martina - joined them and hogged Dallas as she wittered on about social capital and ignored him completely.

When she'd gone, Dallas explained the unofficial quota system, whereby 'piney's got affirmative action as they were scarce and should be helped into positions of visibility and influence. 'But that's not ... equitable, is it?'

'Life isn't equitable, Ted. Never was.'

He thought about the Tortoise and the Hare, and then remembered the carry on at County Hall when they'd 'enabled' some learning, disabled Guinea Pigs to work in IT. Talk about systems failure. They'd had to move them into the Care Management team, where they made perfectly competent social workers, as long as they were not allowed anywhere near the computers. But he was desperate to cop off with Dallas and kept this to himself. Any affirmation from that quarter would be quite acceptable.

On arriving at Joe's they reached a circular building. Inside was a reception area with a desk and several youngsters chasing about the place. He sidestepped a small hippo moving at speed in their direction and passed through the main door into the sunshine. Dallas asked him to bring 'Sonny Boy' back. He didn't like kids but had to let her see he was really child tolerant. The wretched boy saw through him straightaway and called him a 'noncer', then burst into tears when Ted shouted at him. The lad's mother, a great lump of indignant affront, was waiting in reception when they came in. 'Was that you bawling at my little bo?'

'I was concerned. I thought he was in danger.'

'Only danger he's in is from blokes like you.'

'Excuse me?'

'Don't you start on me - nasty temper you've got, buster - we've got a zero-tolerance policy on male aggression here.'

Dallas reappeared with someone he recognised. 'I'm just sorting something out with Rose here, then I'll be with you.'

Rosealea nodded at him blankly and turned away, down

one of the corridors. Ted was fed up with this, none of it was his fault. He noticed that Mummy's little treasure was still hanging about. 'Where's your ma gone?'

'Group ferpy.'

Ted smiled and they went for some male bonding over a computer game. It was called 'Spiders from Hades' and was very therapeutic.

'Wayne's World' operated from a lock-up garage at the back of Woodville Industrial Estate. It was run by the Barkers, a colourful family of red setters who were in the business of removals, furniture repairs, small motor jobs and general re-cycling of anything left there for too long. It had been a slow week, so Wayne Barker was glad to get the call from Robert Bear. A price had been agreed and Wayne was commissioned to bring his old transit van to Rosealea's for 'mid-afternoon'.

'You are sure we'll have time?' asked Mr. Bear.

'There'll be three of us - should be alright.'

'Listen Robby, I'd better take things easy. I never bargained for this. You'd have thought the lass would have been made up, not turn her Hog out like she did. She often like that?'

Robert thought about it. 'No, not really. I think the baby coming like she did winded her a bit.'

'Aye, like as not. Often takes 'em that way.'

Did it, thought Robert, *and what way?* What was the old fool on about, was he drawing on the wisdom of years or just talking random rubbish? He didn't really mind though, as all his training and experience had taught him that respect for one's elders was often about listening politely to any amount of fatuous twaddle. Or re-hashed portions of an older and revered tradition of piffle. He could generally see the point of it, as it must have applied in days of yore when the gates of hell were open night and day, and sweet was the descent, easy was the way. You'd need your faith in the old twaddle then, but not now, not when men might fly to Redcar or galvanise day centres. 'What do you mean, Dad?'

'Hormones. Funny things - never touch 'em meself.'

Robert laughed. 'Is that the problem with Nana Bear then?'

'She's just ga-ga and won't take enough water with it. When she lived over at Weeping Willow Farm, I had to go across many-a-time to sort her out.'

Robert dredged up some murky memories of Nana's farm: coldness and a dirty cup, a scabby knee scraped on a chair. Impetigo and lumpy settees. 'The place was a state; wasn't she taken to court in the end?'

'No, we managed to avoid that.'

They fell into a wry exchange of barnyard memories. The day she shot the moon, when the chimney collapsed, Dan the Horse. Eventually, he told his dad he was missing Rosy and the baby. They sat together on her sofa and fell asleep.

A pair of penguins and a tiger cub had joined Ted and his new chum and were pestering for a go with the computer game. He tore himself away and remembered Rosealea, then Dorcas appeared but blanked him as she walked past. He was getting fed up with feeling like a dangerous intruder who must be tolerated, before trouble could erupt. Perhaps he was the only adult male in the place? He stood outside the main entrance. There was nothing doing, so he walked along the side to the buildings rear till he came to an open window and hesitated. He heard voices; one was giving up a nursery doggerel of 'erbert erbert' and the other belonged to Rosealea, who was saying, 'yes, that's right, Mummy's little egghead.'

'Little Phoebe's a darn miracle.'

'Regular genius so they say - can't be from his side though.'

'Is Robert a retard?'

'No, just behaves like one sometimes.'

'How d'you mean, honey?'

'Oh, I suppose we're our own worst enemies. I mean, I always dreamed I'd find the perfect lover, but Robert turned out to be like every other man in Woodville.'

'Is there such a thing, the *perfect* fella?'

'No, but he could try a bit harder, with his yeller kecks and anti-oppressive what sits.'

Ted had heard enough and shouted 'bollocks' quite loudly.

The ensuing silence was unmissable, then Dallas poked her head through the frame. 'Say Ted, what gives?'

'My temper with Princess Piggy in there - that's my chum, my buddy - she's dissing.'

Rosealea's snout appeared next to Dallas, making her seem even more beautiful. 'I wondered what you were doing up here, Teddy.'

'Just listen to the way she talks to folk. No wonder they get fed up with her, and that baby – Robert's little 'un - learning nowt but cheek and wrong words. Call yerself a mother ...'

''Why, Ted, I had no idea you were such a traditionalist.'

'Ted wazzock blubl erbel.'

Rosealea suppressed a laugh and took Phoebe off. 'Come on you, time for your astrophysics.'

Dallas looked at him thoughtfully. 'Old Robert's your buddy right, your chum?'

Ted felt like drawling 'sure is ma'am' but settled for a soft 'yes'.

'Listen, meet me out front in ten. I got an idea.'

She pulled the window closed so he wandered over to the fence to calm down and watch the industrial estate. A dirty white van was swaying gracefully along a pot-holed track to the main road. He knew from experience that you could only be yourself in love.

From the driver's seat of his van, Wayne Barker looked back across to the fenced-off building and shouted 'bastards'.

The first thing he saw when he got back to reception was Phoebe asleep in her buggy with two white rats keeping an eye on her - no doubt in case of any men. Rosealea appeared and the Rats were keen to push the baby outside.

'Maybe tomorrow,' she said.

'They're cute,' murmured Ted.

'Their father's getting sentenced tomorrow. Were all hoping for life, worse than a human.'

Dallas joined them. 'Hey, you guys, time for our rap.'

They followed her to a smaller room fitted out with bean bags and uncomfortable sofas. Ted thought the place could do with a visit from Linda Barker, the thinking man's Kirsty Chick. They made themselves comfortable.

'Rose and me have been talking'—*you don't say*, thought Ted - 'and we agree that some soft rock ad hoc off the wall rapster remedies are what's needed in these here parts. You dig?'

'Not really,' he answered as Rosealea looked away.

'Okay, what you need to do is get your old chum to haul arse up here with you in tow, and then the four of us can thrash this thing out.'

He looked to Rosealea, who gave him a neutral shrug. 'When should I bring him up then?'

'Just bring him right on up, without the old Daddyo.'

'Er, right. I'll nip then.'

. . .

Wayne parked his van outside Rosealea's house at half-past three and Robert met him with his best matey had-it-all-to-do front. It was all the same to Wayne; he simply wanted to know how much clobber there was to shift. He got a good idea when he went inside.

'What a site ... does anyone live here? We'll have to get some stuff out before we can get to business on this job. Someone a bit tapped live here then ... we're not going to find 'em under a settee, are we?'

'Nothing like that,' stated Pa Bear. 'Just a small misunderstanding.'

'Okay ... well, let's start with that wardrobe, then we can swing some of the other stuff.'

Robert's father appeared. 'Tell you what, Dad. You be in charge of what's going or staying while me and Wayne set to, eh?'

'Right enough, lad.'

Wayne Barker was used to this - the way perfectly normal Woodville folk decided to become swarthy men of work. He never knew whether to be flattered or offended.

ELEVEN
EASY LIVIN'

With Ted in love and Robert knackered
Great men say what really mattered
Will the Hawk outpace the cheetah
Boss Grogan get a new gas meter?

DALLAS POKED her beak round the door at Joes Garage. 'Okay, Guys and Dolls, will luck be a lady tonight?'

Rosealea looked at her with only mild irritation. 'Actually, I think we'll be fine - from here on in.'

'Okay, then Mr. Bear the second, saddle up and get them doggies rollin'.'

Robert felt a second's doubt about whether he really did want them back,, but he was concerned that he might shout at Dallas if he had to listen to any more of her Texas twaddle - so in a way she had brought them together. And he was sure it was what he wanted.

Rosealea picked up Phoebe. 'So, I think that's it, Dallas. We're off home.'

'Good, I'll leave you to it - gotta be on time for Ted.'

· · ·

'Is your stuff ready, Rosy?'

'I'll go and sort that out; you look after Phoebe. What about all your clobber from the house?'

In Wayne's van. Shit. 'All sorted.' Herbert.

Left alone for the first time with his daughter, he sensed the anxiety Rosy had told him about. The fact of Phoebe felt awesome. They weren't allowed to die now. She was just beginning, and he was thinking about the last things; he began to cry, then he saw that she was fiddling with something behind one of the chairs.

She was coughing and making a chokey sort of noise. He picked her up and saw she was gagging on some old chewing gum and that she would die in his arms. He saw the heartrending turn out at the funeral, the long barren months as he and Rosy tried in vain to find a reason to believe, the separation and bitter middle years. And always and forever the scalding image of the poor bairn hacking up her precious life in his arms. Hacking up a concussed Woodlouse which settled wetly in a generous gob of phlegm on his wrist. He wiped her mouth while the Woodlouse came to and struggled free of the clinging posit.

'Pwaah,' said Phoebe.

'Not keen then,' said Robert.

'Cheers, mate,' called the Woodlouse as he made himself scarce under a chair.

'Would you like something to eat, eh? Nice chewy stick?'

'She's not long since had her feed,' said Rosealea, struggling in with bin bags on an old trolley.

'Is that all ours? You were definitely travelling light when you left on that Terry creature?'

'Oh, you wouldn't believe the clothes they've got here.

Some of them are brand new. It's better than the Save The Saps charity shop up the town. I'll have to wash mine and return 'em but Phoebe can keep her own little treasure - a tiny kimono just like Chinese Lils.'

'That reminds me. I saw Tiger Lily up the precinct. She was saying something about the old Professor, about him being poorly still. I was never completely happy with the way that was left. You know, assertive outreach went out and when he wouldn't answer, they closed the case as he wouldn't engage. Then, when we flew over the place going to York ... do you remember Trevor, the little chap with the powered lino? A queer place right enough ...'

'Rob, Phoebe wants picking up - give her here, then stash the bags.'

'Oh, I've not brought Firefly. We came in a van.'

'That's even better. I'll see if anyone else wants a lift.'

'No, don't do that. It's Wayne's van and he's taken his lot home in it. With my gear in the back.'

'You stupid ... great Herbert.'

Phoebe showed some interest. 'Erbert erbert wazzock.'

'Will you stop calling me that?'

'Don't shout at the baby, twit face.'

'I was shouting at *you*.'

'You've upset her again; she doesn't know what all the noise is about, do you baby? See what you've done now. A fresh start, I don't think.'

Just keep thinking hormones and being a precious drama queen. He considered the rackety upbringing. Muck on the carpet, six to a bed, the father a waster the mother an old sow and no bonnet to call her own. It was no wonder she could be a bit rough and ready. 'I'm sorry babe, it's all been a bit of an upheaval.'

'Tell me about it – yes, darling, I know. Don't you fret. Dad's going to sort it all out for us.'

'Right, is there a phone I can use?'

'Just round there,' answered Rosealea as she pointed to a short corridor leading away from the reception area.

He was glad to get away for a while, even if he didn't have a clue what to do. He was determined not to bother his dad, so he phoned Willie Mouse. His manager gave him the number for a mini-cab firm and some avuncular advice.

'Listen, lad, it's no good her going up there every time she's not suited. A man must prevail - call me old-fashioned, but they'll dance a merry tune if you let 'em. I'll say goodbye.'

Pissed again thought Robert and phoned Lex Bedlington. The woman he spoke to seemed to know all about Joe's and asked him if it was the last chance saloon car he required. Or, if it was his first time, would he like to open an account with them?

'Listen up, Mrs. Lex, this is just a one-off misunderstanding, not Virginia Wolf. Can I hire some transport or not, eh?'

'Our drivers are all trained in anger management, Mr. Bear.'

After making his needs plain, Robert put down the phone and wandered away from reception, towards a pile of wood being supervised by his nephew, Wilbur. The flamboyant youth was still smarting from his earlier encounter with Robert. 'What are you doing here, Mr. Macho? Come to take the piss?'

'Listen I'm sorry - in a bit of yellow wood at the moment.'

'What you on about now?'

'It's just a saying - something to do with being lost and not knowing which way to go.'

'Right.'

'Anyway Wilbur, what's all this? It looks very interesting.'

Wilbur took his time. 'It's going to be a sculpture, a piece in wood. I might paint it yellow. What brings you up here?'

'Oh, I'm here on work.'

Wilbur nodded, told his uncle to let Mrs. Bear know he had asked after her then wandered off. Robert thought that dafter folk than Wilbur had made a life for themselves in the arts, but had they made a family work?

'There's a cab coming, we'll get all our stuff in easy.'

'Good - here she wants her dad now.'

Phoebe was an odd-looking baby. Robert reckoned that, seen from the side, she could pass for a dwarf seal pup but that was out of the question once she rolled on her back. When they got home, he decided she was tired and that he should put her down while Rosealea inspected the place. She wouldn't kick up while the baby was settling for the night and learning how to say 'Dad'.

Downstairs, Rosealea was setting to rights a few minor issues with the soft furnishings while she enjoyed the sound of Robert crooning 'Up Up and Away (In My Beautiful Balloon)'. She went up when he mouthed 'nearly gone off'.

She smiled to herself as Robert tiptoed theatrically from the crib with pursed lips.

'Maw dud,' said Phoebe.

Rosealea asked him how big his repertoire was and went back downstairs. After quite a bit of 'Saturday Night Beaver', she heard the stairs creak and stood up to hug up as he came in. They stood together by the door for a long time.

'I'm sorry, Dud,' said Rosealea eventually.

'It's alright,' responded Robert and they sat together on the settee where they listened for any sounds upstairs. This highlighted material coming in from outside: kids playing in the back field, birdsong, a back door closing somewhere. 'I can remember those noises from when I was a Cub and I had to go up when it was still light. Do you remember that Rosy?'

'There were so many in and out of our little house, you got used to sleeping through anything, and the only time my father ever sang was hours after we'd gone up ... loudly.'

They sat closely as the light went. Robert thought about one of the Prof's better ideas.

The wayward savant had invented the Clunkatron, a kind of recording machine able to collect the random sounds of street life and notate them so that musical composition emerged. The Prof claimed this as a new musical form: Clun-klumpenmusick.

He was known to have studied composition in Germany and certainly knew a thing or two about knocking up machines, so when he let it be known that he had put together sundry valves in an oak cabinet, some forgotten recording equipment and his own unique talents, the world was ready to sit up and listen. When he announced the premier of his 'Woodville Fantasy' at the Town Hall, the tickets went like a flash. Everyone had wanted it to work and, in some ways, it had. As a piece of absurdist theatre and there'd been many laughs but not with the artists. The Beaux Arts Ensemble had been under-rehearsed for such complex music and never got to grips with its swiftly changing forms. When part of his specially made Clunkmeister fell off during the 'song of the worms' interlude, he lost his cool and told the audience to go outside and hear for themselves, and collect a refund on the way.

'What you thinking about, babe?'

'The Old Professor. Remember his days as a composer?'

'Barmy old sod - is he off on one again?'

'I don't know. Anyway, shouldn't we value diversity, work with difference?'

'If you say so. We're probably in for our share of that with sweetie-pie.'

'Is she really going to be some kind of genius? She catches on sharp enough.'

Rosealea gave her partner a fond look. 'This consultant chappie should be able to tell us more.'

'Do we have to have him, Rosy?'

'No, but I think it would be a good idea, save us getting referred to social services.'

> The old professor an external assessor?
> It's more than Rose can credit
> She thinks he's just a daft old josser
> And what's more she's good as said it.

Ted had attended the recital of the Prof's new music and thought the decision to abandon it had been hasty. He'd passed up on his refund and tried to console the composer by reminding him of Stravinskymouse's first night with 'The Rite of Spring' and that the public needed time to get the good stuff. He remembered it as he sat with Dallas in a dodgy club at Toddling Town, absorbing the bracing sound of Archie Sheep's band. At least the Prof's stuff had been piano; Sheep and crew uncorked an almost physical impact. The wallop packed by two trombones, sax and drums was dished out with a casual violence and sounded nothing like Miff Mole. After the first arrangement, a polyphonic rave up called 'Incident at Catford', he turned to Dallas and asked her what she thought.

'Wow,' she said. 'Hit me, baby, one more time.' Loud enough for the band to hear.

Archie, a gangling Congolese Meercat, smiled and led the group into a slower, not unpleasant piece called 'Groanin'. This included some raspy singing from the drummer who came over in the intermission to say hello. He was a swarthy Slow Lorris called Philip who'd recognised Dallas' drawl and was happy to meet someone from 'back home'.

Ted wasn't exactly frozen out, but he could grasp only a small amount of what was said and a lot of the communication was conveyed in facial expressions, hand signals, and for all he knew, some kind of Texan ESP. He'd never felt so fogeyish and buttoned down, like the scruffy rector of Puddingdale amongst glittering creatures from the fast life.

He cleared his throat and took orders for drinks. On his way to get them in he heard Dallas' dulcet chimes asking 'ain't he sweet'? There was a crush at the bar and Ted struck up with a fat Tabby Cat from the town who told him that Archie Sheep's records gave you no idea of the visceral effect of a live performance. He'd also called Ted 'man' and asked if anyone was with 'that American bird'.

Ted spotted space opening up and left the cool Cat to it. When he got back to their table, the drummer had gone, and Ted fussed over the surplus drink. Dallas told him to chill. Ted sat down and felt a proper twit, then the band came back on for their second set. He was glad when it had finished.

'Darn tootin,' said Dallas. 'So, Daddyo, what'dya think of that?'

'Plenty of tooting but—'

'Didn't you love the force and energy, the crashin' and abangin', and what about that Cat on the trombone?'

'What was that quieter tune called?'

'Oh, I don't know, Ted baby, but we gotta loosen you up. Let's you and me take a walk.'

'Good idea, it is quite warm in here now.'

. . .

'Rosy.'

'What?'

'Can you hear Phoebe?'

'No, she's asleep.'

'Is she alright though?'

'I should think so; go and have a look if you like.'

'But won't I wake her up?'

'Probably. You've woken me up now.'

Two minutes later he was fast asleep, and she was wide awake trying to remember the number for Joe's Garage.

TWELVE
A TEDDY BEARS' PICNIC

It's party time at Roberts' place
The cream of Woodville's invited
Rosy's put on a pleasing face
Their way ahead's well sighted
But who can know the futures trace
Can wrong turns all be righted?

BOB WATSON HAD BEEN FAR AFIELD on his night flight, staying over at a mate's nest in Forest Town. Refreshed and keen to get back home, he set off before first light. As he drifted silently through trees behind a line of scruffy buildings, something caught his beady eye. He came to rest on a large shed, from where he saw sudden movement. He half hoped for a Field Mouse convention or another abandoned haul of dead rats, so Bob was puzzled when he saw bulkier forms lying together beneath rough sacking. He recognised Ted Sloth, Robert Bear's chum, but the other figure from what he could see was a gaudy looking creature, and unfamiliar. He didn't want to intrude and took off into the night.

. . .

At the Professor's castle, an insect was hanging loose in the master bedroom. Nobody ever cleaned the place and it had become a kind of new town. Thick webs lined the closed curtains while dead flies roasted on the ledge, groaning 'eat me'. Indolent Spiders were of no use to the Old Professor though; like recalcitrant Woodlice or can't-be-arsed Silverfish, they had to earn their place in the castle of discovery. The crusty egg head was not alone; in a small truckle bed at the other end of the bedroom lay the little fellow with the tasseled cap, which perched on his sleepy head at a jaunty angle.

The Spider - Graham Lister - mocked him as 'a big twerp' and scuttled across the carpet towards the secret message machine, which was tapping out an incoming call. Lister pulled himself up to the printer and had a look. It was an important wire from Woodville General. He lost interest and settled down in the Professor's silvery side hair. There were generally rich pickings to be had.

Robert's granny was restive. By the time she'd creaked downstairs and rattled some pots and pans, so was Robert's mother. She got up to join the older woman for a cup of tea and they got to talking – about Woodville's bin collection policy, laxatives, wills, and then a loose connection from Nanna took them to 'our Robert'.

She was full of concern. 'Need to smarten his ideas up with that one now. Leading him such a dance - nowt like that in our day, when I brought you home and Grandpa Bear says, "reckon she'll do" and went back to work. Couldn't afford to take time off then.'

'I generally remember me dad as a gentle man, always played with us.'

'He was but there was none of this song and dance about everything. You've been soft on that lad and now he's got a pantomime dame on his hands. She'll want more than talking to will that one - mind that little bairn's a treasure. Takes after our side with her brains, of course ... but fella me lad has it all to do. This tea tastes like soap! Is it that new stuff they've got in? I don't care for it at all.'

Mrs. Bear knew she'd soon blow herself out, then need only simple care management for the rest of the morning. Just like Robert in his pram. He was often an early riser too.

'Dud dud wazzock - blah blah blerbert.'
'She's getting there; it's a wise child eh?'
'Eh. Yer what?'
'That knows its own father - you going to see to her then?'
'Erm, yes ... yes. You mean, right now?'
'She'll want changing. You'll find the stuff over by the cot.'
Fine, he thought. I'll do it. You have a lie in.

Across the tracks at Toddling Town, the outhouse of desire held signs of life. On an improvised bed of corrugated iron, canvas and sacking, two tired lovers stretched and spooned. She looked at him. When the morning sun caught his tufty head, he looked to her like a beautiful mole coming up blearily to the new day. She pulled him closer.

'You gotta be tired, honey. What happened to all that British reserve?'

'Yes, well – oh, what a night, eh?'

Dallas laughed and asked how long they had till the bus

back. 'Tell me some more of that stuff from lives of the poets. I just love listening when you serve it up.'

Ted showed himself to be a bookish lover as he pleased her with lines from Walter De La Mare, Thom Gull and Marianne Moorhen.

'Who's that oddball guy - wears bicycle clips and plays with himself nights?'

He knew she meant Philip Starling but didn't want to sully their little bower with talk of dead horses or myxomatosis. He told her the bus was due, so they dusted themselves down and hit the road.

Robert was getting the hang of bringing up the baby. Changed and full of stir-about, Phoebe showed some interest in a Woodlouse on the windowsill. He picked her up carefully and took her for a closer look but the naughty Woodlouse shouted, 'bog off' and scarpered.

It didn't matter as baby showed more interest in what she could see of the back garden. Father had an idea. She would be ready for another sleep and it was a grand morning, so he lifted her into her buggy and chattered fondly about whiskers on kittens and not to disturb Mummy. He parked her by the back window. He reckoned he'd earned a cup of tea.

He was just shaping up for his first sip when the front door rattled. He dashed through and was surprised to see the Old Professor's sawn-off assistant in the front garden.

'Fess is in back – lookeesee, Mr. B.'

'Pardon?'

'Special mission - we fly in big bird. Is top secret.'

'Hang on, you can't just ... '

At this point, from somewhere near the top of the house, Rosealea screamed and then enquired where the 'effin ell ee' was. He ran upstairs and she struck him on the head then pushed him to the window. In the garden, the Old Professor had cradled their baby in his arms and was walking down the lawn towards his mighty serpent, who was pawing the ground and snorting.

Robert and Rosealea were rooted to the rug, unable to move or speak as the Prof held Phoebe up to the beast, as if in offering.

Robert pulled open a window and bawled out, 'Bring her back here, you stupid old twat! And then prepare to be punched - and tether that pissin' thing in the back lane. Go on, Professor Pernickety Daft-as-a-Brush.'

Rosealea was impressed and told Robert to 'give him one from me'.

But by the time he'd run downstairs and wrenched Phoebe away from the interloper most of the fight had gone and he was just glad his sweetie-pie was alright.

'He's very good with children, you know.'

'Who is?'

'Beausephalus, my trusty steed.'

'Aye well, maybe when she's a bit older, eh?'

Then the Professor's friend showed himself from around the side of the house as Rosealea came downstairs. 'Ah Guido,' said the Prof. 'I'm glad you're here ... '

'I came with you, Boss, on the giant newt...'

'Not 'im an' all. Why don't you just move the day centre to our back garden? They'll all be here soon - every fruitcake in town,' declared Rosealea.

The Professor tried to help. 'I see, dear lady, that you have recently hatched this remarkable issue. Your internal balance will not have returned to its former equilibrium, your waters are a storm-tossed channel of realignment. Perhaps some of my settling powders—'

'You're on about my hormones aren't you, you silver-tongued man of science?'

'I don't care to be spoken to in that way.'

'Well pop off then, slap head.'

This amused Guido, who took off down the garden to see to the newt with heaving shoulders.

'Let's start again, eh? Phoebe's alright and I'm sure we'd have been better prepared if we'd known you were coming. That right, babe?'

'I'm not having him in the house.'

'Well,' said the Professor, 'it's a fine enough morning. Perhaps we might sit in the garden, but hasn't Guido explained? We come with big news from the infinite cave of Hippocrates. Imagine my thoughts when—'

'Give over, mate - spare us the fancy talk, eh, and get Giuseppe to take that great lummox out the way.'

The old boy had enough sense to follow Guido down the garden, where they lingered for further orders.

'What's cracking off, Robby?'

'I've no more idea than you. The little fella appeared at the front door and the other two were already out the back, thank you very much. I'll give 'em a bit longer then; we'll get the full SP.'

Rosealea smiled at him and rubbed his arm. 'I heard you setting him to rights.'

Robert walked with certainty towards the back field and Rosealea took Phoebe upstairs to watch from the bedroom window. 'Life's never dull with your dad.'

'Pufesser daf beggar.'

She sat on the bed and laughed into Phoebe. When they went to the window a conference was in session by the bushes.

The Prof. was standing with his arms akimbo, listening to Robert, who was making emphatic gestures and looking towards the house. Guido was watching from the serpent's back. A neutral observer might have expected a minimalist Morris Dance to break out, but Robert finished speaking, and the Professor had his say. Guido then produced a sheet of paper from his tunic.

Robert came in and spoke to his wife in the kitchen. 'Sit down, Rosy, this concerns us all.'

'Sounds exciting, eh, babe. Go on then, lover.'

'You know they want to monitor Phoebe, study her wondrous workings and all?'

'Yeah, but what's bonkers and short arse got to do with it?'

'Just hear me out. This might not be as daft as it sounds ... just hear me out, babe, and be a bit nicer to Guido, he's a top lad really.'

'You what, that pair testing our little treasure? Do you really think I'd hand her over to those two eedjets?'

'Rosy, calm down. Phoebe picks it all up, you know.'

'Perfeser djet.'

Robert explained. It seemed that the hospital consultant was a pal of the Professor's. He had been astonished when, as a medical student, he'd come across the Professor's ground-breaking study of crossbreeding in potato weevils; this had been done in his youth and paved the way for a general theory of miscegenation in small creatures. Rosealea was too disturbed by what Robert was saying to object, so he was able to tell her more about the distinguished work with small creatures. Naturally, the old boy had been a gifted child and therefore able to understand others and their ways.

'He told you all this, did he?'

'Some of it - Willie Mouse knows more.'

'Bollocks, man.'

'Rosy, please.'

'Perfess bollks.'

'So, what's he want then?'

'Have I to ask him in?'

'Alright, but his funny friend can mind the beast, eh?'

Robert was surprised that Rosy would have the Old Professor in their home but reasoned that she generally preferred to shout at people from the comfort of her own living room. He cautioned the visitor on the way up the garden path, but the Prof. assured him that he knew what he was doing.

Rosy briefed the wonderbabe. 'When Dud brings perfess in say hello. Good girl.' She positioned herself in a comfy chair with Phoebe on her lap, secure in the knowledge that Joe's Garage was only a motion away.

'Right,' said Robert. 'Here we are, Rosealea and little Phoebe.'

Mother gave Baby a little stroke. 'Hell bollok.'

'Oh, please, call me Albert.'

'Herbert Herbert,' cried Baby and waggled her little hands.

Robert was mortified. 'I'm so sorry, she's just learning her words.'

'It's quite alright. I visit many unruly homes in my occasional work for the Health Board.'

Rosealea laughed, making Robert wonder what was wrong with her. The Professor sat down and explained. Much of the fieldwork would be carried out by the parents, and some by Phoebe herself. It was to be recorded within the parameters of some 'simple formulations' and a 'reflective journal', which would take up just a few minutes every day.

The Professor would visit each month to see how things were going, then every three months a more formal examination would take place up at the castle. A special 'Kindersuite' would be built, and it would be fun for all concerned. It would be important work; he would be available at all times and Phoebe would be entitled to special vouchers for Motherbare. People like her came along but once in a generation and had much to tell us about the wonderful but sometimes puzzling world of things and stuff.

He padded this out with tales of similar studies in unlikely spots. There was mention of the Saltburn Merboy, which gave Robert a chance to talk about their eventful trip to the North East. The Prof. agreed that this was an odd, untamed region where he had once spent an evening and had seen many things. He then bored them into submission with a digest of the potato-weevil study, which had apparently opened an unknown door to the natural world.

Phoebe had dosed off and Rosealea seemed unusually peaceable throughout the seminar. In some ways, Robert had been fascinated by the Prof. He appeared unfazed by any connections to his previous encounter with them and seemed to be not of their world. But then again, he wasn't. The very few humans who prospered in the natural world were always interesting. Some, like the obnoxious Gaffer Jarge, found the challenges and demands of adaptation too much and regressed to an archetypical lumpeness, while others went to the reservations like the one by Boss Grogan. Here, they were sometimes ogled at on Sundays by the cheeky Monkeys who lived in the trees overlooking the compound. Robert's own favourite sap had been Mrs. Ritchie, who'd sold flowers at the edge of Waggoner's Wood and lived in a boathouse by the pond. She sold a lot of flowers because she chucked stones if you passed without buying. There'd been a great hooha when she'd snuffed it the previous winter, but the council said you couldn't blame social services for the weather, and it had all been forgotten.

Rosealea was laughing again but nobody had said anything funny. Guido appeared at the back door. 'Tell boss is time we were off; Seph is cross, and I want my lunch.'

'Tell him I'm coming,' called the Prof.

Robert asked Guido why the serpent was cross. The local ducks had decided he was a visiting duck God and wouldn't leave him alone. He'd threatened to eat them so they'd produced a mangy old mallard as a sacrifice and he'd felt he couldn't back down; now he felt ill and unable to fly. Robert was alarmed that this could mean they'd be stuck with their visitors and decided to do what he could to speed the departing guest.

Phoebe was burbling away happily on the Professor's knee. Robert scooped her up and told him the transport was having an anxiety attack.

With its passengers hanging on, the snorting serpent pranced round the field several times before charging the hedge. It only just cleared it, then climbed steadily above the house. Robert caught a mental snapshot of the scene and the Professor's demeanor. It dilated in his memory to include a vague picture of an inscrutable Guido and the old Prof. with an expression of startled resignation, a helpless acceptance that the cross serpent might just as easily put them down in the middle of Woodville Lake as do as it was asked. With his lank and silken locks waving in the wind as they disappeared,

Robert thought he was a reckless nitwit tinkering with forces he had little hold over. A holy fool. A well-intentioned menace. A Herbert.

'What do you think his full name is Rosy?'

'I'm sure Phoebe could come up with something.'

'Dud sing.'

'Over to you, Val Pelican.'

Robert took Phoebe back out to the garden and gave her 'The Bright Elusive Butterfly of Love' then 'The Birdy Song'. He looked back to the house at one point and saw a smiling Rosealea watching from the kitchen.

In another part of Woodville, two new lovers had the back seat to themselves on one of Barry's Buses. Dallas was resting her small head on Ted's shoulder. Her morning after mode of demure attachment was bringing out something noble and potent in him. He'd already chatted knowledgably with Dave the goat, who was driving them, about the best routes around Nutbush City, helped Mrs. Lamb with a troublesome basket and chuckled fondly at a pair of young sheepdogs who wanted to talk to Mrs. Lamb.

Dallas yawned and told Ted they were cute as she planted a chaste peck on his shiny nose. Ted felt like Nutty, the old King of Woodville, who could pull up trees as he spoke poetry. He'd never known a lass like Dallas before, from rutting hellcat to pliant soulmate and, who knew, back again before teatime. He suggested they call in on Robert with a nice present for the baby.

They duly presented themselves with hearty hellos and a junior glockenspiel.

'That's so kind,' said Rosealea and embraced Ted. 'We should have a party - now in fact, eh?'

'Oh,' said Ted, 'I was hoping for a quiet night tonight. There's a programme on about social exclusion. It sounds very interesting you know.'

'Wow, Ted, why don't we get in some bottles of apple cider and play Turkey in the Straw? Dull city, eh Phoebe?'

'I just thought you'd prefer a quiet night, you know - get settled in again.'

'How about a housewarming?' asked Dallas.

'Who were you thinking of inviting?' asked Robert.

'Lighten up, sober sides,' scoffed Rosealea. 'It's not time for the last waltz yet, old chap.'

Robert felt perturbed. 'What's got into you, Rosy - why are you talking like that?'

'Listen to yourself. It's the inspiration of the moment that counts, go with the flow.'

Dallas and Ted had taken a tactful interest in the top end of the garden and Robert was remembering the time he'd let the flow of inspiration go over the soft furnishings. Something wasn't ringing right with Rosealea.

'Are you feeling alright, pet?'

'Yes, why?'

'Well ... you're not yourself. You're all skittish and, er, tolerant.'

'And?'

'And it's not normal for you. I'm not complaining, not as such. I just can't help noticing.'

Rosealea looked up at a balloon and waved to the pig passing by in the basket. 'I should think it's this stuff one of the women at Joe's put me onto.'

'What stuff?'

'It's called goofy dust. You sniff it up and life doesn't seem so bad. It really goes for Pigs, on account of our snouts and hardy sniffing. I only use it now and again.'

Robert gasped and took the baby away from its delinquent mother. 'You're on drugs. You're peering over the parapet of vice into the murky world of sin. Are you an addict, a regular user?'

'Not as such.'

'Good, because it's a short bus ride from the world of murky sin to the blasted plains of abandon - the flophouse and the gutter. I've heard—'

'Robert shut up! You're making me laugh.'

'Oh, don't listen to me, I'm only the father of your baby, the baby of wonder, remember?'

'Listen, Chucky Egg I'd never let it get out of hand. I can go whole days without it. We're not going to end up defrauding the council or exploiting vulnerable citizens - apart from you.'

'Yes, well, it's all been a bit of a shock.'

They watched Ted and Dallas for a while. They were talking to one of the cows in the back field and looked very nice together. The cow was called Yvonne and she was a Ukrainian singer. Robert wondered where Dallas might be leading Ted next. They turned back towards them. 'Hey, now I gotta hear this Gertrude Stein of the glockenspiel.'

Robert drew a confused Ted back down the garden for a blokey chat and Dallas began to teach a delighted Phoebe how to play 'I'm Just A Girl Who Can't Say No'.

'What gives, old man?' asked Ted.

'Rosealea's on drugs. That Joe's wants closing down ... not Grogans lot.'

Ted had to think on his feet. 'Well, at least you're back together and most people grow out of drugs sooner or later.'

'Are you soft or what - just think about it! Rosealea on hard drugs?'

'Is she on them today then?'

Robert was exasperated. 'Yes, as a matter of fact she is. Haven't you noticed how agreeable she's being?'

Ted looked back in the direction of tinkling chimes at the top of the garden. Robert's daughter was tapping out a free-form improvisation while Rosealea was chatting with Dallas. She looked quite normal, not listening to The Jimi Hamster Experience or lost in another world of substance abuse. It was him that was drugged, mind altered on the lurve drug. Old Robert needed to hang looser in the saddle.

'I didn't know what to make of it at first. It takes some swallowing; I'll tell you that much.'

Ted gave him a curious look. 'You mean ... you as well?'

'No, you twit, the news, the info, the sapping cosh of revelation that my wife is in thrall to narcotics, and God knows what else. Wait till my granny hears.'

Ted was thinking that his overheated colleague could do with some of the stuff. 'What is it anyway - that thing The Beetles used to sing about HMV?'

'It's called 'Goofy Dust', obtainable at Joe's Garage and most respectable voluntary organisations. Your doxy should know all about it.'

'Ah yes, I know all about this. Bev Linnet from dual diagnosis told me all about it - a stash hit the streets the other week. It's meant to be quite harmless, inducing mild euphoria and disinheriting for an hour. They're keen to find out where it's coming from though.'

Robert despaired afresh at the notion of a publicly disinherited Rosealea, then had an idea. Where did every crackpot enterprise and harebrained caper in Woodville originate? He also remembered what Tiger Lily had mentioned about him being radio rental again. He was a public nuisance and had to be regulated, certainly before he started his study of Phoebe.

Ted was more cautious. The tale he heard pointed them in a different direction - the Loose Connections day centre for the elderly.

Robert scoffed but heard a queer tale unfold as Ted explained.

Since the cuts removed all the care staff, bar one - an idle guinea pig called Jason - the 'users' had been 'given the opportunity' to run the place for themselves. Jason generally opened up, then left them to it. Well, they hit on a recovery type project all their own, taking an interest in people's earlier experience. You know, writing stories even giving illustrated talks - nothing like the poker or who-am-I-today games they used to get. One day, a retired chemist had brought in her box of tricks. The next week, a former tobacconist brought in some ancient stock which included a sizeable, sealed tin with laughing skull and crossbones emblazoned on it. Then the fun really started, when the powders in the tin were carefully evaluated and a small dose put in Jason's tea. He sang them an hours' worth of opera, then went to sleep.

Robert looked out over the field for a while, then said. 'My gran goes to that day centre.'

Dallas sashayed down the lawn. Robert couldn't help noticing what a fit bird she was or wonder what she was doing with Ted Sloth. Woodville's Mr. Nembutal. It didn't ring right.

'Hey fellas, we're having a party - a house-warming, baby-welcoming, wham-bam, thankee-kindly, ol-boy type of function. Come and join us.'

'Why not?' asked Ted.

'Whatever,' said Robert, seeing a chance to hang loose.

'Swell, now think up your guest list because Rosy's gonna get a cherub to pass it round.'

Robert tightened up at that. Pigs and cherubs had not had happy relations since her uncle's disgraceful cherub shoots, but whatever. Dallas went back to the infant prodigy who was picking out 'Greensleeves'. He was certain she was augmenting the chordal structure of the tune deliberately. 'Good vibes Bub,' he called.

'Dud dud nobbin' hud.'

Dallas asked him for another traditional air and he suggested 'Anarchy in the UK'. 'Don't believe I ever heard that before.'

'You're not missing much,' said Ted. 'What about "Roll Me Over in The Clover"?'

'Can you teach her a jazz one?' asked her fond father.

'Yeah. "Oo Bop Shebam" – okay, Phoebe, let's shake this one down.', Robert could see he'd be meeting some new people as well as modern jazz numbers.

When he got back to the house, Rosealea was talking to a cherub in the lounge. She was introduced as Furzer and seemed different from the simple specimens he was used to. She was wearing a balaclava instead of the traditional flower petal and heavy work boots, with a scruffy combat jacket. It turned out that she was affiliated to Joe's Garage and active in a radical cherub's group. She would get her mates to distribute invites if they could come too.

Rosealea reciprocated by telling her where her uncle lived.

Furzer looked Robert up and down, then took off through the open window.

'Right,' said Rosealea. 'Nip down to One Step and get some of that nice rough lager and some crisps. We can get the party started here and now.'

'What about Phoebe?'

'Your Gran's on the list.

'That means they'll all be coming. Your lot too?'

'Why not?'

The do got going as soon as the host returned with the goods. Phoebe was watching Dallas play the vibes and learning new words from Ted, who had warmed to her. Lager was taken and the party began to get a shine as the first guests arrived - a party of ducks he knew from Parks and Gardens, who took their drinks down to the rhododendron and yapped amongst themselves. Then a more familiar face - Boss Grogan - appeared with a party from the day centre and Wayne of the van and complex family. Wayne handed over a six pack of 'Nutty' and asked Robert how it was going.

'I dunno - alright, I guess. How about you?'

'T'same ... rock steady for a few months, then they usually forget, eh?'

Robert pondered, then said, 'If you say so, mate.'

Wayne nudged him. 'Listen, our lass has brought some stuff with her; fancy a blast?'

'Why not?'

Back in the house, Rosealea and Dallas were chatting with Robert's mother. She was dandling Phoebe on her knee and quoting freely from the new edition of 'Granny Knows Best'. 'If she gets a bad chest, fumes from a smoky fire will clear it and if she should fret at bedtime, the book of common prayer should

calm her. Most important of all - if she should spit out her food
...'

Dallas jumped in to rescue Rosealea, who was still reeling
from the image of Granny wielding a prayer book at a fretful
infant. 'This is fascinating, Ma Bear. I did my dissertation on
the mothers of Toodleallyboodle in the Blue Ridge Mountains.'

'Oh, yes, and what did they have to say?'

'Keep the bowels clear, the wine cellar cool and ward off
smoky fumes.'

'Well, that's mighty fine, Missy, but I think you'll find we
march to a different drummer here in lil' old Woodville.'

Rosealea had to look at the rug and Dallas, for once, was
lost for a sassy quip. Instead, she brought the battling Granny
up to date with Phoebe's prowess on the glockenspiel. A brief
recital for later was promised.

'Is that right then?' Granny asked Baby.

'Yep,' said Baby.

Rosealea raised the issue of Woodville's nutty Professor
and his possible role in Phoebe's childhood, stressing that this
would not interfere with as normal an upbringing as possible.
Dallas added a rider about Phoebe's importance to future
generations of women. Banty had appeared and put in that
women had the hands that rocked the cradle and dealt the
cards.

''Appen,' said Mrs. Bear and asked what food was on.

Banty explained that most folk had brought something, and
a 'grand spread' had resulted.

'Well, lass,' said Granny. 'Let's have a good pick before the
men start.'

'I just love those tribal elders,' gushed Dallas. 'They've
forgotten more than we'll ever know.'

. . .

Outside, the party was swinging. A portly cat had turned up with a string bass and Dallas was telling a stoat with a banjo about the chords she wanted 'behind her'.

Christ, thought Robert, *she's going to sing*. Where was Ted?

'Alright, cus?'

'Hello, Wilbur, how's it hanging - I mean going?'

'Your ma about, Roberto?'

'In the house.'

This really was Woodville. Wilbur was wearing a full-length antique gown and what Robert understood to be a fascinator. It was an untidy production in rough grey material, and the general effect was of a large gob of tailored snot. He watched his nephew go and wondered what had happened to the lad who used to throw stones at the gypsies with him when they were carefree men of the forest?

He opened a fresh can and wandered down the garden where Wayne and Guido were sharing a splif.

'Hey man,' called Wayne. 'It's good stuff this, from the Professor's personal stash. Have a toke, Rob.'

'Er, perhaps later. Is the Professor here, Guido?'

'Boss very busy. Take off into the night on Richard and drop me off on way.'

'Richard?'

'Our mighty serpent - he go like stink.'

'Oh, right. He seemed a bit fractious before; is he alright now?'

'Yeah, boss thrash him and say he is a duplicitous and ungrateful fellow. Good friends again now.'

Wayne cracked up at this and lay down to 'watch the planets man'. Guido joined Wayne and showed him where to look.

Robert decided to get pissed.

· · ·

Ted and Boss Grogan were sitting with Dorcas on some old gardens at the front of the house. Boss was explaining the plan to save the centre. It was a daring and risk-laden wheeze which depended on some involvement with the saps from the compound nearby. Wilbur and Dorcas had already engaged a few of them with lager and chairs. It had been a difficult task as the saps kept quarrelling and weeing everywhere but, eventually, they'd managed to get three of them to sit still and agree to help. They would get all their friends and stage a sit-in at the centre and sing 'We Shall Not Be Moved' until Boss told them. They would also make as much noise as they could and annoy everyone in the neighbourhood. It would go on until the council promise to keep New Leaves open and donate some arm chairs to the saps.

'Are you sure they'll do what they're told?' inquired Ted.

'No,' replied Boss. 'But County Hall will be appalled, and the press will have a field day. You can see the headlines now: 'Are We Human Or Are We Bonkers?', 'Freddie Star Ate My Day Centre'. Elected members don't like that sort of thing.'

'Who's the councilor for the ward?' asked Ted.

'Bob Tench,' said Dorcas.

'I don't think I know him.'

'Stood on a 'Fish against Fascism' ticket against Councilor Gull and won. He's never been to the centre.'

'Dallas is a sort of gull, you know,' said Ted.

'She's a sort of something,' stated Dorcas. 'But she's been a real shot in the butt for the centre. We're really going to miss her when she goes back to the States.'

Ted's foolish heart skipped a beat. Why hadn't he worked that one out? But it was alright, wasn't it? Lovers were always being divided across distances, tossed and tested on the stormy seas of something or other. He just hadn't bargained for it yet, that was all.

Then he caught Dallas' nasal wail coming through the babble. 'I feel the Earth move' she sang. 'I feel the sky tumblin' down ohohoh yeah'.

Ted thought he'd been a fool to do her dirty work ... *but not anymore, baby. That aint me babe* ... or was it? He had some thinking' to do, oh yeah.

Robert's Mother and her Mother were admiring Wilbur in the living room.

'That's a lovely dress, our Wilbur,' said Robert's ma. 'You really know how to carry it off - it goes perfectly with your colouring.'

Granma Bear reached into her capacious handbag for some 'snuff' and commented that it was queer how the older styles were coming back just now.

Robert's father closed the door on his way out. He needed the company of other fellows, not women, and Wilbur. He could see why the youth stayed indoors though; he'd be very cold in that dress when the temperature changed.

Otto and Lottie had turned up with Willie Mouse and plenty of 'Blue Monk' Belgian beer. Otto cautioned that it was 'most strong' and should be sampled carefully. Mr. Bear collared two bottles ('one for my pal') and went off down the garden.

'Does Robert's father have a drinking problem, Herr Mouse?' asked Lottie.

'Not a drink problem.'

Banty scuttled over and told Lottie that Phoebe was about to play something on her chimes. Lottie was familiar with Klangfarben melodies and thought she caught orphaned traces within the ill-disciplined soundscape. She wondered if they were playing one of Stockhausen's better known tunes. As she approached, Lottie saw Ted, sober-faced, at the back of the group, enjoying the music. She waved but he didn't notice and moved into the shadows where vague shapes moved together.

Lottie felt disapproving but stirred.

Dear reader,

We hope you enjoyed reading *Robert Tries to Help*. Please take a moment to leave a review, even if it's a short one. Your opinion is important to us.

Discover more books by Mike Pearson at https://www.nextchapter.pub/authors/mike-pearson

Want to know when one of our books is free or discounted? Join the newsletter at http://eepurl.com/bqqB3H

Best regards,

Mike Pearson and the Next Chapter Team

Robert Tries To Help
ISBN: 978-4-82414-991-6

Published by
Next Chapter
2-5-6 SANNO
SANNO BRIDGE
143-0023 Ota-Ku, Tokyo
+818035793528

9th September 2022

Lightning Source UK Ltd.
Milton Keynes UK
UKHW040035221122
412610UK00003B/55